Penumbra

A Zombie Bedtime Stories

Collection

Quantronics Press

www.PlanetThea.com

ISBN: 978-0-9877347-5-4 (paperback)
ISBN: 978-0-9877347-6-1 (ebook)

To my mother. You are more awesome than you know.

Zombie Bedtime Stories, part 1:

Locked In

The ambulance raced down the quiet residential street, sirens blaring. Potholes rocked the vehicle from side to side, and the car ceding the right of way before them was exciting. It was a beautiful summer morning, and most of the rush-hour morning commute had died down, leaving the roads open and easy to navigate.

Haley was a newly minted paramedic, and she rode in the passenger seat on the way to their latest call. Having been on the job for just over two months, she felt prepared for anything. She liked helping people, and had been a candy striper in high school. While being a paramedic was demanding, she enjoyed the challenge and the rewarding feeling that came from saving lives. She even liked her partner Frank, no matter how much he pretended the feeling wasn't mutual. Their destination was a park across the street from her old high school. Haley was secretly excited to see how much it had changed since she'd graduated. She fondly remembered the park benches that had been claimed by different cliques, especially the hours spent after school reading under the giant oak tree in the center of the park. She also thought of the many friends that she had made there, and how she had befriended the little kids who frequented the monkey bars and swings. She had even been known to hang upside down from the ancient and rusted monkey bars while preschoolers squealed in delight.

As they approached, Haley could see multiple police cars, fire trucks and a few other ambulances in the distance. Flashing lights danced along the horizon. Frowning, she turned to her partner Frank. "Do you know what's going on?" she blurted out, forgetting that they seldom knew the true extent of a situation before arrival.

"They're throwing me a birthday party, duh." Haley instantly regretted asking and went back to staring out the window.

They emerged from behind a fire truck, and Haley's jaw dropped in astonishment. She could make out a small, thin frame dressed in rags fighting with a group of police officers. She immediately recognized the assailant; a local homeless man who went by the nickname 'Buddy'. He had been befriended by many high school students over the years, Haley among them. Small, terrified children who were barely school aged had climbed to the top of the monkey bars, and a bloody group of teenagers were being triaged by other first responders. The three burly police officers struggling with Buddy couldn't keep him pinned to the ground and fought to keep him under control. The tallest of them had at least a foot of height on Buddy's minuscule frame. Haley hesitated as they exited the safety of their vehicle.

"Oh my God, that's Buddy! He's that homeless guy I told you about last week!"

"Wow. Sure looks harmless to me. You *fed* that guy?" Frank said, his voice dripping with sarcasm.

"I don't understand how he could snap like this." Haley said, turning to Frank, who was a veteran in the service. He'd served long enough to have seen everything.

Frank also took great pleasure in being an insufferable curmudgeon.

"It was only a matter of time I guess, what with the mental hospital shutting down and dumping them all out on the street. Like that guy who thought he heard voices and killed that local reporter. Those damn kids weren't helping any by treating him like a pet and feeding him scraps from their table!" the middle-aged man offered, his voice more gruff than usual. Haley bristled, feeling immediately defensive. She'd chatted with Buddy on occasion, going so far as to smuggle him food from her parents' house from time to time. She couldn't see any harm in what she'd done, even now.

"I really don't want it to be *us* that take him."

"Don't worry about it, Haley. A job is a job." He paused then, and then shot her a rare smile. "You'll do fine. Just keep your head on straight, Rookie."

Frank's face returned to its usual scowl as they walked toward the group of teenagers, gurney in tow. A fair-haired girl of about fifteen shivered under a blanket, despite the fact that it was a warm summer morning. An older boy held her close against him. His hand was pressed against the stain that was seeping through the blanket over her shoulder. His own arms were scuffed and displayed superficial bite marks, but he seemed oblivious to his own condition as he whispered calmly in her ear in an effort to puncture the terror and hysteria that still possessed her. The others were distant and brooding, covered in scratches and abrasions of varying severity. The students flinched and cowered under the barrage of Buddy's howls, while the younger kids marooned on the monkey bars screamed for help. Haley missed a step, and held onto the gurney for support. She could not comprehend the extent of the injuries and carnage caused by one small man.

"Why?" the girl stammered after she'd choked back another body-racking sob. "Why? Why?" Haley fought the impulse to hug the injured girl, sensing her veneer of professionalism was stretched almost to the limit. In her head, she kept repeating the words: *I need to be strong. I can't help them if I'm upset* like a meditative mantra.

"Can you walk? We're going to take you to the hospital and get you checked out." She offered in an attempt to ease the girl. "Everything is going to be okay," Haley added as she extended a hand to the girl.

"He's loose! Look out!" voices cried out. Haley spun to see Buddy charging towards her, his face pasted with grime and blood. He screamed like she'd never heard before in her line of work (and hoped to never hear again). It was so far removed from the gentle, soft voice she remembered.

Haley threw up her arms as he made a lunge for her face. His unimaginable strength pitched them both to the ground. The blow winded her. Her eyes widened in alarm as she squirmed under his wizened form to keep his decaying teeth away from her flesh. His fetid breath was tinged with the scent of blood, the overwhelming stench burning into her lungs. Haley thought she was going to vomit. The three officers and Frank shouted as they struggled to gain control of the crazed man. Deafened by Buddy's shrieks, the terror of the cacophony threatened to paralyze her. A Taser was drawn, but its discharge barely seemed to jolt Buddy, prompting a renewed flurry of attacks. Haley felt a discernible electric tingle pass through her own body, so she knew the device had worked, but on the wrong person. With this realization her thoughts became frantic and incoherent. As she felt her arms weaken from the exertion, she couldn't help wondering if Buddy was drugged.

She screamed, and then kneed him hard in the groin. Nothing. She kicked, dodged, and twisted herself to keep from being bitten; her instincts urged her to fight back, to escape, to kill. As her sense of helplessness grew, she could not free herself and she was tiring rapidly. She begged between frantic gasps for air "Don't hurt me! Please Buddy, it's me, Haley! Stop! Please!" her cries faltering as she ran out of breath.

After what seemed an eternity, a burly officer caught Buddy in a joint lock, heaving her attacker off the ground. Buddy flailed, and his dirty hand swiped her face, clawing desperately at the air. She cried out as his jagged fingernails tore through her skin. Her hand rushed to the left side of her face. She could feel the burning swell of angry, bleeding skin. Frank's usually dour expression was touched with concern, and he extended his hand to help Haley to her feet. Overwhelmed by sobs and terror, Haley watched the group of police officers working to subdue and restrain Buddy, who had lodged his teeth in a Kevlar vest and was unable to chew his way out. She gulped down air as Frank pulled her away from the fight.

"He got you real good, looks like *you're* our victim for this call. After that, I'm taking you home, and I want none of your tough crap. There are other teams here now - they can deal with the kids." Before she could protest, Frank was rubbing a stinging salve into her wounds, forcing tears down her face. "Come on, it's just a little saline. You're getting jabbed next, at the hospital." Sighing, Haley wiped her eyes and hoped that nobody else had seen her cry.

Haley's ordeal at the hospital was a waste of time. After being subjected to another unnecessary abrasive facial and a few needles, she was relieved to see Frank waiting for her at the end of the hall. She forced a quick smile, the stinging in her cheek made it difficult to look cheerful.

The drive home was quiet. Wrapped in Frank's jacket, she was shivering and cold and her insides resounded with anxiety like a piano whose keys had been violently hammered. The event played over and over again in her mind. Buddy's frenetic but empty eyes. The Taser. No response to a full-strength knee to the genitals. The scratch. Her wound burned more as she thought about it. It was like the infectious memory of the incident had invaded her mind, and she could think of little else. Haley couldn't believe what had happened. It defied logic. She had always known Buddy as a gentle, though very dysfunctional man. Having been unable to adapt to life outside of the institution, he had taken residence around her old high school. He had often been compared to a lovable crazy uncle by the student body because of his insane tall tales and fatherly yet crazy disposition when interacting with the students he befriended. His behavior was polite and friendly, always happy to listen to the troubles and aspirations of the students. He was known to have occasional outbursts and innocent paranoid ramblings, but Haley had never observed that behavior first-hand. Haley recalled him being very interested in her volunteer work – candy striping at a nursing home. *He always asked me if there was room for him. I should have helped him get somewhere safe.* She shook her head and fought the guilt which had emerged from the dark corners of her mind. *This wasn't my fault, that was years ago.*

They pulled onto her street, and she noticed her boyfriend's car in the driveway. Jake worked a typical day job, and it was barely mid-afternoon.

"I took the liberty of calling your boyfriend. You're off for the next couple of days. Get some rest and clear your head." He handed her a business card for a local therapist. "Give her a call if you're worried about coming back to work. Less has spooked the most seasoned medics away from the job, and I *hate* changing partners."

"I'll be back, don't you worry. This is nowhere near as bad as that time we found that junkie's dead mother in his bathtub and he went nuts on us. Thanks for the drive, Frank." She said as she fumbled for the door handle.

"Training won't prepare you for reality," he went on "or getting jumped by a nut case that you once thought was a friend. Take care of yourself Rookie, and if you need help, ask for God's sake. And mine!" He laughed hoarsely. "Now take it easy, and that's an order, kid!" he said, waving her off.

The door unlocked, and Haley stepped out of the car. Reluctantly, she drew off Frank's jacket and tossed it in the passenger's seat, exposing her lean frame to the warm breeze. She walked stiffly to the patio doors of their modest duplex, finding it already unlocked. The rich aroma of freshly baked cookies overtook her. She could see Jake, her tall, clean-cut man with angular features and warm blue eyes standing down the short hall, in the kitchen. He smiled, but his sharp eyes and strong features revealed concern as he strode across the floor to embrace her. When they met in the landing to the kitchen, Haley's anxiety receded as he drew her head to his chest for a long hug. After she pulled away, her attention was drawn by a simple mirror which hung on the wall across from a group of neatly framed family pictures. A short series of steps lead up to the rest of the home, past the utilitarian kitchen Jake worked tirelessly to keep spotless.

"Frank called, I came home right away. I didn't want you being here alone." He pursed his lips as he took in her delicate features, eyes drawn to the scratches on her cheek. Haley turned her head, feeling self-conscious and gazed into the mirror hanging behind Jake's shoulder, brooding. "He really got you," Jake said, as he ran a hand gently down her back "Is there anything I can get you? I picked up some beer on my way home." He locked his gaze onto her, attempting to distract her from the mirror.

"It was so freaky. Nothing stopped him, I felt so helpless," she said, rushing through the words "I don't think it will scar. That would be the worst." She said as she experimentally stroked the scratches on her face and winced at the stinging pain.

"Do you want to talk about it, sweetie?" Jake asked, stroking the back of her neck. She turned away from the mirror to look at him.

"I want to get my mind off it. I keep going over it in my head, and it's making everything worse. Maybe later."

"I'll be here when you're ready." He kissed her forehead, his lips hot on her cool skin.

"Where did you get those cookies?" She said, changing the subject, turning to the large dish sitting on the table.

"That was Mrs. Jones' doing. She caught me coming home early, and I told her that you had some trouble at work. She turned up thirty minutes later with a bunch of cookies she was baking for her grandson's birthday."

Haley smiled. Mrs. Jones was a sweet old lady, and a tireless busybody. But she meant well, and always looked out for her neighbors. A widow, her life revolved around her grandchildren, and had taken a doting interest in the young couple, often bringing them treats. Haley often helped her with her vegetable garden on her days off. Despite her nosiness, Mrs. Jones was a good neighbor.

"She's the sweetest lady ever! I'll have to go over and thank her." Haley was ravenous, having skipped lunch because of her ordeal. "But right now, I think these cookies and I have some business to take care of."

"Leave some for me!" Jake said as she snatched up the tray from the kitchen table and headed in the direction of the living room.

"Make me!" She said, laughing as she set them on the coffee table.

"You win. Frank already told me what happens to guys who get fresh with you, and I don't want to sing soprano."

With a lopsided grin, Haley grabbed a cookie and drooled in anticipation. Mrs. Jones was a baker of masterful skill, and she savored its enduring warmth in her hand, and the tantalizing smell. She took a big bite and gagged. It tasted like some kind of nondescript hardened paste, crumbling and spreading its dull blandness to the rest of her mouth. *Did she forget the sugar?* She picked up the tray and carried the cookies back to the kitchen.

"Something's wrong with these cookies. They taste like crap!" she exclaimed. Jake's expression was one of puzzlement.

"I snuck one earlier, they taste great." He grabbed a cookie, and took a bite. "See, it's good, you're just tired babe."

"I was sure they were bad." She said, perplexed as she stared down at the remaining cookies, dull aftertaste still lingering.

"Don't push yourself. Go lie down. Don't do anything until you're ready. How about I order us a pizza? My treat."

"Okay. Get a meat lover's will you?" The words slipped out before she could think. Pizza choice was usually a point of contention because she'd always maintained a staunch preference for vegetarian toppings, while Jake insisted on a more carnivorous selection. He brightened at the suggestion, but hesitated for a moment.

"Sure. Now go lie down before I pick your ass up and carry you to bed! We can talk later, when you're feeling right." He finished.

"Okay, okay!" she said as she left the room. She felt disoriented, not herself. *It's just stress. I'll give the therapist a call in the morning if sleep doesn't help.* She curled up on the couch, pulling her favorite old quilt over herself. Sleep came quickly, but it was a listless, disturbed slumber and she found herself waking frequently, shivering. At sunset the doorbell rang, and Jake arrived with a steaming hot pizza.

"Hey, you're up! Good timing, pizza's here!" He said, as he cleared some papers from the coffee table. Haley sat up, and was disgusted at the sight of the meat-laden pizza.

All that grease! Jake passed her a slice, which she seized and ravenously sucked the toppings off, discarding the slimy crust. She hurriedly reached for another slice, but focused only on the cheese and meat before she crammed the greasy mess into her mouth.

"You know, I don't really think this is what they mean when they recommend low-carb diets." Jake said, still on his first slice.

Haley paused momentarily, confused. She was insatiably hungry; the meat was barely making an impact on her intense hunger.

"I skipped lunch, remember? I'm so hungry!" She said, feeling very defensive, hoping he'd drop it. Unconsciously, she reached for another slice, and its mangled sauce and cheesy grease ran down her face. She couldn't explain why she was neglecting the crust, or why the cookies tasted terrible. *My body knows what it needs. Sugar is bad for you. Clearly I need protein.*

"Have a napkin cutie, you're being so gross! Leave me some." Jake snickered to himself as he selected another slice. By the time she finished, Haley had demolished the top layer of over half of their large pizza. She felt nasty and bloated, but the hunger lingered. Walking to the fridge, she opened the door and gazed inside. Snatching her jar of dill pickles, she fished one out, drawing it to her lips. Taking a sharp bite, she enjoyed its satisfying crunch. When the acrid, sour taste filled her mouth, she dropped the jar which smashed on the floor. She retched violently. A long trickle of mucus dangled from her lips as she heaved. She was dizzy, confused, and her body was almost paralyzed by a creeping cold that was overtaking her extremities.

"What happened, are you alright, babe?" Jake asked, running into the room. She looked up at him, her wide green eyes bloodshot and teary, shivering from the cold. She wiped her mouth quickly to eliminate the evidence of the accident's cause. He stooped over the remains of the pickle jar to gather up the larger shards.

"I just got dizzy, it was nothing." She said, afraid to be perceived as insane. "I'm going to bed, I'm sure it's just stress, or shock or something and I'll be better in the morning."

Jake nodded. "I'll clean this crap up," he said as he frowned at the spreading puddle of pickle juice on the floor. "You get to bed. I'm taking you to the hospital in the morning if you're not better, okay?" He sounded suspicious, his brow furrowed in the dim refrigerator light.

Haley drew herself to her feet and went to brush her teeth. Her hands were shaking, her left eye twitched, and she used her hand to support herself against the wall as she walked. The small nightlight in the bathroom cast a dim light down the hallway. Once she turned on the light, the large bathroom mirror displayed how pale she had become. The fluorescent lights accentuated her sunken eyes. *It's just stress, I'm okay.* She repeated the litany as she gagged on the toothpaste and examined her angry red scars in the mirror.

She changed into thick flannel pajamas and some thick wool socks and crawled into bed, hoping the twitching would subside. She pulled extra blankets over herself and curled into the fetal position. The shivering slowed, and she slid into a deep, unbroken slumber.

Haley woke to the bright morning sun beaming in her face. She felt a dull ache in the back of her skull, and was consumed by grogginess. She sat up, the motion mechanical yet foreign, steadying herself on the side of the bed as she jammed her feet into slippers. The smell of pancakes and bacon filled the air. She was ravenous, and hoped Jake made lots of extra bacon.

She made her way to the stairs leading down to the kitchen, her stomach curdling with intense, painful emptiness. Jake saw her and beamed a smile. "I hope you're ready for some chocolate chip pancakes!"

Haley tried to speak, but her mouth flapped noiselessly, and she continued towards the stairs. Walking as though the incline didn't exist, Haley helplessly tumbled down the short flight of stairs, and lay sprawled on the landing, stunned. Her hands shuffled from under her as though they had a will of their own. Jake rushed over to help her up. Haley had taken those stairs thousands of times, and could not understand why she hadn't stepped down.

Focused on the pain in her legs and tail bone, Haley was unaware of her hand stretching upwards and snatching Jake's outstretched arm just above the elbow, a strong jolt of energy pulling him off-balance. A deep, throaty growl escaped Haley's lips, snapping her out of her stupor and into the horrifying reality that she was no longer in control. She tried to cover her mouth in alarm, but her arm wouldn't move.

There was little time for alarm, because with a deadly grace she had flipped Jake onto the floor, pinning him under her weight.

"What are you doing? Get off!" he screamed, terror rising in his deep voice. This force which had gripped her made her stronger. Haley found that she was unable to stop the events that were unfolding. She pleaded with herself to stop and regain control. Her efforts were futile.

Her face shot over his chest to his throat, lips curling back to reveal straight, white teeth. Striking, she tore into his throat, the sudden wash of coppery blood flooded her mouth. His arms flailed, pummeling her shoulders in a desperate effort to free himself from her grasp. *Jake, stop me! I'm so sorry. It's not me!* Her mind cried out with the shrillness of his screams, and his spasms as she hewed chunks from his body. The life drained from him as her form continued its feast. Haley was transfixed on his open, dead blue eyes. *No, no, no!* She screamed to herself, trying to stop her cannibalistic gorging. Mouthfuls of meat were ripped from his exposed skin, and Haley was forced to watch as she tore off his handsome face, one mouthful at a time. Her inner despair was so deep that she had ceased to taste his flesh, overcome by guilt. Smoke filled the air as the sizzling bacon began to burn.

Her reverie was interrupted by a knock on the patio doors. Haley recognized Mrs. Jones' voice through the glass.

"Is everything alright? What was that screaming? Hello?" She called in, knocking on the glass. However, whatever Haley heard, so did the monster in control. It turned from Jake's shredded corpse with an unearthly shriek and ran towards the noise. Haley felt a blunt pain as she crashed into the doors, and hoped that the glass would contain her, and keep Mrs. Jones safe. Blood smeared over the glass. *Run! Get away!*

"Haley! Are you okay? Where did the blood come from? I'm calling 911" she yelled through the glass while she backed away from the door, eyes wide behind thick glasses. The phone in the kitchen began to ring. She could not answer. She was intent on her prey.

Backing up, the monster screamed as it rammed Haley's head through the patio door, and her mental anguish over the loss of Jake was interrupted by the agony of sharp glass slicing into her scalp and scraping her forearms, thick blood oozing through her hair and dripping from her fingertips. Mrs. Jones' petit frame rushed towards the gate as Haley's body broke through the door, intent on continuing its feast. The stinging of her wounds was dulled by the appalling anticipation of what was to come. The ringing stopped, and the phone went silent. She contemplated what she had done, her terrible crime.

Catching up to the diminutive old woman with ease, Haley could feel palatable waves of terror emanating from her neighbor. Dread filled Haley as she anticipated the bloodshed that was about to begin. Bones cracked as she tackled the tiny woman, and a shrill wail followed. *Listen to me! Stop!*

Again, her possessed body attacked the neck, a whiff of sickly-sweet perfume assailed her nostrils as her incisors tore paper-thin skin. The now familiar taste of blood filled her mouth, pouring from Mrs. Jones' wounds. From her grotesque vantage point, Haley determined that she had hit the jugular and that Mrs. Jones' suffering would be short. *You made me cookies and taught me how to garden. You don't deserve this.* Haley heard shrieks and cries, jumbled with sirens in the distance. She wondered if they were coming to take her away.

A long time passed until her body finished consuming its vile feast. Her stomach still growled with hunger. She stood, and ambled towards the street. Haley tried to assess the situation. Pulpy bits of flesh were stuck between her teeth, and the slices in her arms and scalp oozed and burned. Blood-soaked pajamas clung to her body. *This isn't a nightmare* she realized with a shock. It's all too real.

Talking an aimless route through deserted suburban streets Haley noted with satisfaction the drawn blinds and empty playgrounds. Helicopters flew in distant skies. She was hopeful that nobody else would get in her way until she figured out the situation. She knew she wasn't a monster by definition. *It's like I'm in a coma. I need to wake up, or send out a message.*

The taste in her mouth was disgusting, she was nauseated. She concentrated on the sickness until she vomited a bloody sludge all over herself. The taste was vile, but she saw an opportunity to regain some control. She wondered if she had indeed induced vomiting. This fed her determination to regain control. She focused harder, willing herself to blink, to hold her breath, to stop walking.

Not long into her efforts, her elation evaporated as a figure approached in the distance. Walking with a slight limp, he hobbled towards her. Drawing closer, her heart sank as she took in the tall, blood-soaked man with vacant eyes that looked through her. The smell of rot and decay hung around him, and he silently walked alongside her. The damning implication that there was another like her shattered Haley's optimism, and forced her to contemplate the terrible possibility of escaping – only to be eaten herself. Her grim pessimism was alarming, and she wanted to cry. She was crushed by intense guilt over the deaths of Jake and Mrs. Jones. She couldn't get their anguished screams out of her mind. *They cared about me, and I killed them.*

A police car pulled up alongside them. The windows were tinted completely black, and she was unable to make out anything inside. The officers did not leave their vehicle, but followed at close range. Her body appeared not to notice, nor did her companion. She re-doubled her efforts to break free, trying to send a signal to the officers. *I only attack if it looks human, or sounds human.* She desperately wanted to be rescued. She was heartbroken over the deaths of Jake and Mrs. Jones. They had both died trying to help her. The guilt was too much to bear.

Her heart sank as the car sped off. The sound of sirens grew louder. Haley saw a roadblock up ahead, partially finished. An officer was standing outside his car with his back turned, speaking frantically into his radio. Her partner growled, she hissed in turn. They charged in unison, her companion oblivious to his injuries. The officer only realized what was happening when it was too late. *I can't close my eyes. I don't want to watch!*

Like two hawks, they descended upon the man, fingers grasping like talons. They tore into him, their synchronization applied with deadly results. Seizing an arm, Haley bit through his shirt at his left shoulder while pushing his head back to expose the throat. Her partner wasted no time in attacking their victim's throat, chewing through the windpipe and silencing his screams. While rending flesh from his arms, Haley hoped that the officer's partner would return and shoot them both.

After leaving the flayed corpse and still running police car, Haley wanted to scream. She saw why the man was distracted from the roadblock. They were defending from an attack on the other side, trying to keep the threat contained in the urban center. A second police officer's body was lying on the ground, surrounded by that of a few bloody civilians, their bodies marred by gunshots and jagged broken bones. Haley kept finding parallels between her situation and a zombie movie. While she knew that zombies were ravenous, mindless monsters, Haley could not accept that she was undead, or mindless. She was convinced she could be cured.

She joined a throng of others, men, women, and children. They were miserable looking brutes, devoid of any expression and stripped of their humanity. The rank smell of blood and decaying flesh filled the air. Covered in blood-matted, tattered clothing, some were missing teeth, fingers, or had gouged-out throats. Haley's medical training told her that many of their injuries were seriously debilitating, if not fatal. Her morale slumped further when she realized that they couldn't stop themselves, even to recover and heal. *I'm not me anymore. Am I a ghost, an echo? How can this nightmare end? Can I end it?*

The swarm of former humanity pushed further into the urban center, only slowing to engulf any human unlucky enough to encounter them. Haley found herself becoming dead to their screams, mired in her own suffering.

The thoughts haunted her. Yesterday, she had been vibrant and happy, infectiously positive and with boundless hopes for life. She had looked forward to buying a home, gardening with Mrs. Jones and starting a family of her own with Jake. Today, she only wanted death. She seethed with anger and despair.

Her thoughts returned to the park and her encounter with Buddy. She understood now that he was trapped, just like she was. The thought disturbed her. Her alarm rose when she realized that Buddy had indeed recognized her and had been unable to stop himself from attacking her. *Just like with Jake and Mrs. Jones.*

A formation of helicopters flew overhead, interrupting Haley's despondent reverie. She couldn't see what lay ahead of them on the road; her view was blocked by the fiends ahead of her. Shrill hissing ahead foreshadowed another bloody melee, and Haley instinctively closed down her mind, blocking out thoughts and feelings. She repeated a mantra to herself - *It's not me. It's the disease. I don't want to be hungry anymore.* It didn't help.

Her concentration was shattered by a hail of weapons fire. The creatures ahead of her surged. They deftly avoided the convulsing bodies of their fallen companions and charged the source of resistance. There was shouting ahead, human voices barking orders and another volley of gunfire mowed down the ranks in front of her, leaving her with a clear view of the front lines. Fear shot through her mind as she took in the blockade protecting an elementary school. Helicopters swarmed over the building, taking off and landing on the roof. She didn't want to kill again, and the paradox was painful to contemplate. The air teased her long, matted hair as she charged towards the men, and the agonizing cuts in her arms re-opened as she ran.

Ahead was a personnel carrier, and a group of several well-armed men in gray camouflage uniforms. All were wearing ventilation masks, and had built a makeshift picket line, guns at the ready. Despite having lost awareness of her heartbeat some time ago, Haley felt a distinctive pause. The seething mass of ruined humanity overtook the outside barriers, and Haley was among the forerunners, shrieking and clawing her way to the exposed flesh of a soldier posted at the front. He fought back valiantly, and his powerful punches dislodged her teeth, causing rattling popping sounds inside her skull. Unexpectedly, she tasted the rot of her own putrid blood. *I am dead! I don't remember dying.*

The realization slammed into her psyche as her decaying essence pooled in her mouth, the pain of the injury overshadowed by the sickening reality that there was no going back. *There is no salvation, no cure, only death. I guess Frank will need to change partners after all.* She hoped the old grouch was still himself.

Another of the undead pinned the fighting man, and two others pulled on his legs, tearing them off with a gory spray of blood and sinew. Her field of view was blurred by the frenzy, but she could hear the enraged screams and shouts of his companions.

"Fall back!" said a deep, powerful voice. "Get that flamethrower up here!"

Fire. They're going to burn me. The notion was terrifying. Having responded to fires, she knew the intense pain experienced by burn victims. *What a horrible way to die.* Woefully, she acknowledged that she'd rather burn than hurt anyone else.

While dismembering the hapless soldier, a surge of motion from behind overtook her, as her fellow zombies pushed forward to attack the retreating men. A dull hissing sound blasted ahead, quickly followed by enraged howls. Intense heat danced on the right side of her body. *Not fire. Somebody help me. Please.*

Her body straightened, and took in the gruesome sight of burned husks smoldered on the ground, some still writhing and in flames. The stench of burnt flesh and hair permeated the air, and the gray smoke heightened the moment, creating a sense of apocalyptic gloom. *I'm sorry, Jake. I'll be with you soon.* She ran, her gurgling screams chilled her to the bone. *Do it, kill me. I don't want to hurt anyone else.*

The tall man holding the flamethrower cocked the weapon, his face hidden by a protective mask. Moments ticked by. The anticipation was agonizing. She expected the most excruciating pain of her life. Haley knew burning would be more painful than the lacerations of broken glass, and beyond losing her teeth. *Could anything hurt worse than killing Jake?*

A bright salvo of orange flame erupted from the weapon, rolling towards her with an infernal fluidity. The searing heat danced across her skin for a split-second, and then seething pain consumed her. Haley's mind blazed with agony and she collapsed to the ground. A strange euphoria overtook her. She was grateful to the mysterious man. Her suffering was over.

Thank you.

Zombie Bedtime Stories, part 2:

Locked Out

Doctor Anna Lewis sighed. Her blond hair was bound in a too-tight bun that made her scalp ache, and freckles sparkled on her pale skin below her hazel eyes. She was closer to forty than she'd like to admit, but she maintained the boundless, youthful energy needed to do her job. She administrated a small, underfunded and understaffed infectious disease research center had been ordered to take on an important, top priority project. She waited in her small, utilitarian office for the courier who would bring the samples and briefing. The morning sun peeked through the window behind her, illuminating the room and the specs of dust floating in the air. Anna was annoyed at the request and the strain it would put on her staff. She wondered if they would have to work double shifts and overtime. Anna didn't know why they couldn't handle the problem at the much newer facility in the capital. She'd heard there was a riot there, but it was doubtful that a riot would affect the efficiency of a world-class laboratory.

She busied herself with endless paperwork, signing off on purchases, reviewing grant applications and various proposals concerned with expanding the facility. She had been in charge of the facility for just under a year. It had been a significant career advancement for Anna not only because it was a prestigious posting, but because Anna was early into her career as a researcher. She attributed most of her success to the brain drain—many capable scientists had already left the country for greener pastures and bigger research grants. Willful ignorance and resentment towards the scientific community didn't do much to encourage the remaining scientists to stay. She was anxious to find out what this mysterious new project was, and if her labs were up to the challenge.

The sound of a phone cut through her concentration. It was the receptionist's extension.

"Hello Lucy, are they here?"

"Yes, Dr. Lewis. They're setting up in the conference room," the girl answered with a hint of tension in her voice. The formal language she used was strange and uncomfortable.

"I'm on my way, thanks Lucy." She got up from the simple wooden desk and locked her computer. A bookshelf dominated the other side of the room—a relic from the past. Anna filled her bookshelf with obsolete text books. She liked to imagine what the golden age of Western science was like, and having a bookshelf laden with reference books seemed like a quintessential part of capturing the experience. For actual reference she used a body heat powered reader that could fold into her pocket. Some paintings decorated the walls, and notes were stuck to every available surface close to her desk. She checked her hair on the way out, making sure her tight blonde bun hadn't frayed and straightened her black framed glasses. She regretted her decision to forego wearing make-up. Freckles stood out along the bridge of her nose. She snatched her notepad and pen from the bookshelf and headed for the conference room. Unfamiliar voices trickled down the hallway, and she heard the buzz and whine of hand-held radios.

Turning the corner, she missed a step as she took in the group of uniformed men. She recognized their green army uniforms, and was taken aback by the crates of equipment, sealed samples and the glare of sunlight that shone through the usually sealed outer doors. Lucy was overwhelmed by the volume of equipment and personnel coming in. Her attempts to keep up with the requisitions and signing off on new equipment were frantic and rushed. A few researchers had ventured out of their offices and simply watched the spectacle, mouths agape. A tall, solidly built man with a powerful jawline and a graying crew cut approached her and extended a hand. Deep lines ran down his face and crow's feet framed his deep blue eyes.

"Doctor Lewis? I'm Major Cartwright. I apologize for commandeering your facility, but time is of the essence and I think you'll agree about the urgency after I brief you." The words were spoken with a trained confidence, but his rapid presentation belied his anxiety.

"You're turning my facility upside-down, I hope it's for a good cause," she said, to keep the interaction cordial and maintain control over the situation. He motioned her into the conference room.

She sank into a high-backed chair while the major fiddled with his laptop, connecting it to their often-difficult projector. There was a pile of adapters next to him. That projector was almost 20 years old, but she hadn't been able to acquire the funding to replace it, or the rest of their decaying computer equipment. Her lead researchers, balding and white-haired Dr. Grant and the spindly Dr. Evans filed into the room, taking seats on the opposite side of the oval table. The old projector finally flickered on, revealing a paused slideshow.

"I imagine you're wondering why we've taken over your labs. Well, we have a situation on our hands. If you've been listening to the news, no doubt you've heard about the riots in the capital." He straightened, pressing a key on the keyboard. A grisly scene played on the screen. Hordes of bloody, battered forms fought with police and soldiers, shaking off any blows and injuries while continuing to advance. "Truth is, this is no political rally. These people are out of control, and we need to determine the cause. The capital has been shut down and is being evacuated, but the surrounding cities are beginning to report incidents of random, yet intense violence." Major Cartwright stood silent as the disturbing scene looped endlessly on the wall.

Anna stared and struggled to process the gruesome, visceral visuals.

"So why us? Where do we come into this?" Anna felt obligated to speak. She needed answers, to glean sense from that scene cut straight from a horror movie. "You have negotiators, police and guns. We research diseases and catalog new microbes."

"Good question. The answer is, we can't negotiate. Every single person we've managed to capture has been violent and completely uncommunicative." The major's brow furrowed as he drew in a deep breath. Dr. Grant fidgeted in his high-backed chair; audible squeaks broke the long pause. "What's more, is that every time we've taken somebody into custody, we've lost control of the facility within twenty-four hours. This suggests to my superiors that this is more than a sudden wave of intense political indoctrination."

Anna stood up and glared at the man. "So you're saying we're looking for an evil bug that makes people go crazy?" The idea was absurd. Anna knew there had to be some kind of logical explanation.

Major Cartwright pushed a button on his remote, and the video loop transitioned into a grotesque photograph.

Limbs were strewn across the ground, flesh flayed from the bones. A torso contained by a green fully-intact Kevlar vest lay nearby, head still connected. The right side of the man's throat was torn open, strips of skin pulled from his face, giving the appearance of a grotesque mask. Burned bodies littered the background. Anna sank into her chair, and fought down the bile in her throat. Dr. Evans spun her chair to the garbage, and threw up. Dr. Grant sat, mute and transfixed. "What happened there?" the old man asked.

"This was the capital late yesterday afternoon, taken from an evacuation point at an elementary school. This man's injuries were caused by unarmed civilians; some of them children," he paused. "I will remind you that tearing off limbs is a feat of strength beyond the abilities of most people."

"Why do the news reports say that there are riots going on, if this is the reality of the situation?" Something didn't add up, and she wanted to know why.

"To prevent panic, we've limited information about the situation. We don't have all the facts. We needed to clear out the downtown core in a hurry, but everyone in the suburbs are being asked to stay indoors. The phone lines are down and fires are breaking out. We don't know what we're up against."

"Something doesn't seem right about all of this. When did it start? Where's the first case?"

"The first reported cases were two days ago. They were isolated incidents, random violent attacks. The subjects were very difficult to apprehended and control. From the few first responders we were able to interview, we learned the subjects were completely irrational and even attacked those close to them. They also appeared to be immune to non-lethal defense methods. One man claimed that he saw one of them get hit by a Taser with no reaction at all." Major Grant flipped off the projector. Anna could still see the grisly image in the back of her mind. She realized that if it was biological, it would make her career. If it wasn't, this would all be for nothing.

"We'll go with that. So, what goodies did you bring for us?" Anna asked with an irreverent smile. Prim Dr. Evans shook her head in disapproval.

The major smiled for the first time, revealing straight, white teeth. His sharp blue eyes locked with hers. "Right to the fun stuff? I can deal with that. We've brought samples straight from the front lines, and some refrigeration units for said samples. I hope you weren't attached to your cafeteria, my technicians are overhauling it as we speak."

"My lunch was in there. What kind of samples are we talking about?" she suspected she knew the answer, but wanted to be sure.

The smile melted from Major Cartwright's face, his jaw settled into a practiced hardness. "Bodies."

Chapter 2

The hallways were cluttered with empty crates, dollies and packing foam. The dim fluorescent lights cast odd shadows across the hall and over the debris, creating a gloomy, claustrophobic ambiance. Anna likened it to a nightmarish distortion of reality. She walked alongside the major through the hall, the familiar corridors twisted and unrecognizable. They emerged from the labyrinth at the cafeteria. A team of men dragged the ancient white refrigerator out of the narrow doorway, unceremoniously dumping it outside the door. The hall was littered with plastic chairs and tables, some stacked and others tossed aside like giant toys. A large silver refrigeration unit gleamed in the middle of the room while the construction workers tore out cabinets and others covered the wide, bright windows.

"A pathologist will be joining us later today. He will perform the autopsies and collect samples for you." A pair of men saluted the major as they sped down the hall.

"When will the morgue be finished?" Anna wanted some clarity. She needed a plan to tackle this ill-defined and nebulous project.

"Finished is a stretch. Functional will be in a couple of hours. It won't be perfectly up to modern specifications, but the sooner we get the samples contained the better."

"We're fighting against time. I will leave this in your capable hands and see to my staff." The major simply nodded, transfixed on a pair of workers who were installing a cooling unit where their television used to be. She began walking towards her office, lost in reflection over the day's events.

Her reverie was interrupted by Lucy and Dr. Grant as she rounded a corner near the main entranceway. Elderly Dr. Grant looked grandfatherly next to the younger staff members, despite not having any children of his own. Lucy was an incredibly attractive young woman, her shoulder-length red hair accentuated her pale, creamy skin. Unlike many redheads, Lucy had few freckles to detract from her sharp hazel eyes. She was carrying a clipboard, and her freshly manicured red fingernails tapped the solid particleboard impatiently.

"Anna! Just who we needed to see. Did you know all of our experiments have been terminated or put on hold? My samples can't just be frozen somewhere. I know what's going on out there, and it's terrible. I realize the humanitarian concerns, of course. But this project is huge to us, and a lot of grant money is riding on the results. We can't just throw them out and start over!" Dr. Grant stumbled through his words. His latest fascination was with a strain of rapidly mutating bacteria, and she understood that it was a very time-consuming project. She knew how important his project was to the facility – she needed to find a way to save it.

"We still have lab space for them, right? I haven't had a chance to review the requisitions yet."

"You see, that's what *I* wanted to talk to you about." Lucy began. "They've co-opted a lot of space, but some of the older labs, like Dr. Jacobs' old digs, are untouched. We could re-purpose that for current samples so we don't lose anything." Dr. Jacobs had been killed in a car crash three months prior, and Anna had been unable to find a replacement. Presently, interns and graduate students occupied some of the unused labs, and they cannibalized older equipment for their own projects and amusement.

There were even more empty labs, but they had been vacant before Anna had taken over the facility. She doubted they would ever run at full capacity unless the political situation improved.

"Okay, so why don't we move our present experiments down to Doctor Jacobs' lab, and we can quickly train the interns and grad students to look after them. That way, we're free for this project, and the kids won't get in our way." It seemed like a good compromise. "We still have time before the samples and pathologist even get here, let's make the most of it and maybe we'll even come out of this mess ahead."

"That would work. I don't think they'll mind a little something to do." Dr. Grant's face relaxed slightly as he pondered the possibility of renewing his generous research grant.

"It'll take time away from their Internet videos or whatever else they do to waste time. I'll call them up, they probably don't realize anything is going on up here yet." A sly smile crept across Lucy's face. Being younger than the rest of the staff, she had a closer rapport with the students.

"I'll get the samples ready to move. I don't want them playing with my bacteria until I show them what needs doing." Dr. Grant shuffled down the hallway to his lab, and left Anna and Lucy at the corner. Anna often wondered if the rest of the world would find their concern over an obscure strain of bacteria ludicrous.

"Anything else I can help you with Lucy?" The girl hovered over her. Lucy towered over Anna, even in her sneakers.

"No, I think that's it. I need to round up some of those army boys and tell them to clean up their mess. Look at this place!" Lucy kept her workspace immaculate, and the slightest variation in her organizational scheme was enough to cause her to become irate. Anna could sympathize with a chronic desire for organized surroundings.

"Get to it. Once we start we won't have time to stop. I'm going to make sure the other researchers are aware of the lab space restrictions and student workforce."

Lucy sighed and walked down the hall towards reception. Anna hoped to make it to her office without further interruption. She needed time to think, and adapt to these new facts of life. On top of it all, her lunch had gone missing, and she felt like she would never sleep again.

Chapter 3

An urgent hunger gnawed at Anna's stomach as she reviewed the lists of equipment that were being installed. The new morgue dominated her awareness; the grotesque images from the major's slideshow still haunted the depths of her imagination. She fought against the overwhelming revulsion that consumed her. Around her tenth birthday, she had witnessed a fatal car crash while on a walk to visit her grandmother. The thought of having corpses in her cafeteria brought those memories into the forefront of her mind. She could still smell the blood in the air, and feel the eyes of the recently deceased staring into her. She had stood, frozen, unable to look away or to run and hide. Anna recoiled stiffly at the memory, and took a sharp inhale. The memory dispersed.

A sharp series of knocks sounded against the wooden door, and resounded through her small office, breaking her concentration. "Come in."

Major Cartwright stepped inside her office. His uniform had become wrinkled and his eyes appeared more sunken and tired than they had during their meeting earlier.

Regardless, he conducted his movements with exacting precision and he stood with perfect posture in front of her simple wooden desk. He briefly glanced at her bookshelf before speaking: "The samples have arrived. However, I require that we restrict access to the pathologist and his assistant."

Anna couldn't contain her relief. "I need to ask. Why are you restricting access?" She asked, hoping that the reason would be concrete enough to be undebatable.

"Our units have had a very difficult time securing these samples. We've lost contact with all units doing sample collection until now." He drew a deep breath, and suddenly seemed fascinated by the recent collection of scuff marks on his polished shoes.

"You mean they grabbed the corpse and disappeared with it?" she asked, incredulous.

"Yes. We want to consider the possibility that whatever their condition is, that it may be airborne." The fine lines on his face deepened into a frown. "I don't like it, but this was the first location we could get the bodies to before they rotted or vanished."

"I'm not exactly impressed." Had their military fallen so far that they couldn't even pick up corpses efficiently?

"Neither am I, but right now my concern is keeping this facility safe, and any potential infectious agent safely under lock and key."

"Why are you worried about safety? The capital is hours away from here." Anna suspected he wasn't telling her the whole truth.

"We went from having a few isolated cases to full scale riots and roaming mobs overnight. Whatever's causing this, it works fast. Also, loyal men and women have gone missing. These are people whose conduct was beyond reproach and that the army can't afford to lose. I owe their families an explanation, damn it. I need to find out what happened!" His practiced composure melted before her eyes. She could see the despair and guilt etched into his face, anguish over the loss of his people. Anna hadn't expected this level of emotional response from him. Just moments ago, he had seemed like a statue, impervious to the world. Now, he was human, and afraid.

"Major, I'm sorry. I had no idea. What's happening is terrible, and we need to take all the precautions necessary," she said, as she tried to diffuse the awkward moment.

"Please, call me Cliff. This facility may be our only chance at resolving—" he was cut off by his cell phone's characterless ring tone. He checked the call display and stepped into the hall. "Excuse me one moment."

Anna could make out little of the conversation, the scream of saws and construction equipment drowned out Cliff's voice. She figured she'd need to work late, and decided she should call her house mate, Trisha, to let her know. Anna considered asking Trisha to bring her some lunch. Trisha, a nurse, usually had her days off during the week and enjoyed goading Anna when she did something absent-minded, especially when she forgot her lunch. They had been friends since they met in biology class during their college freshman years, and had both graduated as part of the class of 2018. Anna had never married, she'd always been too busy with work, or school, or life. Trisha was a widow who had lost her husband, Daryl, a couple of years ago in a hunting accident. After Daryl had died, Trisha found she couldn't handle the mortgage alone, so Anna gave up her small apartment to stay with her. Anna decided to call her after Major Cliff was done.

"Sorry about that," the major said as he stepped back into the room. "Our pathologist, Doctor Lee Walker, and his assistant have arrived. They're being escorted to the cafeteria now."

"The sooner they get started, the sooner this will be over." Anna tried to convince herself that she wouldn't have to see or touch any of the bodies.

"Would you like me to introduce you to them, Dr. Lewis?"

"In a moment. I have a phone call to make first; I need my roommate to bring me some lunch. One other thing, Major Cliff." she said. She wanted to tease him a little, to bring some levity to the darkness of their shared problem.

"What's that?" he said, stiff and formal.

"Call me Anna." she replied, as her laughter shattered the tension in the room. The major chuckled as he stepped out of her office.

Chapter 4

Trisha had been home, and Anna was fortunate enough to catch her before she left the house to work her dreaded graveyard shift. A quarter of an hour later, Trisha rolled by the lab and dropped off a few sandwiches before leaving for the small town's only hospital. Trisha had jokingly reminded Anna that she might like the late hours and encouraged her to give up research for nursing. Anna doubted that would ever be the case, but knew that no matter the job, working with Trisha would never be dull. Hunger sated, she left her office to look for Major Cartwright and the recently arrived medical examiner.

Walking down the halls, she was relieved to find that the cleanup was going well. No longer cluttered, they were lined neatly with excess equipment and furniture. Teams of men in well-fitting green uniforms were hauling away the debris with hand carts. The floor had been badly scuffed, but Anna wasn't concerned. The building was decades old, and some wear was to be expected. She noted Dr. Grant standing outside his lab with a group of four interns. She walked faster while he was distracted, not wanting to get into another debate about experiment relocation. The man enjoyed the sound of his own voice, and it was known that the interns actively avoided him to prevent themselves from being drawn into inescapable hours-long and one-sided conversations. She evaded him, noting as she did that the interns looked less than excited. They shifted their weight from foot to foot and nodded, faces blank as they glanced at other researchers who were talking to military personnel. The familiar community had been fragmented by the foreign influence.

At last, she saw Major Cartwright at the end of the hallway. He stood next to a man she did not recognize. He was a few inches shorter than Cliff, gray hair cropped close to his balding head. Deep smile creases ran down the sides of his mouth, which made his serious facade seem unnatural. He wore simple jeans with a white tshirt. As she walked closer, she could see that thinly framed wire glasses accentuated his brown eyes. Next to him was a mousey younger woman, whose brown hair was cropped short in a shaggy pixie cut. She wore simple clothes, and her expression was blank and unreadable. She hugged her arms against her slight frame.

Cliff saw Anna approaching and waved her over. "Hello Anna. I'd like to introduce you to medical examiner and longtime friend, Doctor Lee Walker. This is his assistant, Heather Richardson. Allow me to present Doctor Anna Lewis, director of this facility."

Anna extended her hand to Lee, his soft skin yielded to a powerful grip. His eyes locked onto hers, and a warm smile lit up his face and eyes. His hands were cool, with a hint of moisture. She shook Heather's hand, noting the icy feel of her skin and her weak grip. Heather didn't maintain eye contact. "It's good to meet you both." Anna said. Heather returned to looking sullen and wrapped her arm back around herself as though she were fighting off a chill.

"Likewise. We're going to begin by extracting and sealing samples, which we will then transfer to the labs for analysis. I'd like to allow access only to Heather and myself, because of the potential for transmission." He spoke with a casual tone, as though he were discussing lunch.

"So you're going to be wearing decontamination suits and taking precautions?" After hearing the details of the other sample extractions from Cliff, Anna was taking no chances.

"We're going to follow normal procedures. Masks, gloves and aprons, that kind of thing." Lee said, then after becoming aware of Cliff's hard glare, he continued "Of course we will take the utmost care."

"We really need to get to work. Stop wasting time," Heather interrupted—her voice was tense and angry.

"Yes, yes. You're right. Go ahead and set up the equipment, I will join you in a moment." Lee returned to his absurd attempt at seriousness. Heather opened the new outer door to the cafeteria and wordlessly stepped inside.

"What happened to Alice, your old assistant?" Cliff asked Lee as soon as Heather was inside the morgue. Anna felt like a third wheel – totally unneeded.

"She's on maternity leave. Beautiful twin girls. I should drop her a line, she's living in the capital."

"Good for her! I hope..." the major went silent, and his cheerful facial expression slumped.

"Is it that bad?" Lee picked up on the unsaid implication immediately.

"Worse than you can imagine. We need to get on this." His tone of voice demanded no room for argument.

"No time like the present. It was a pleasure meeting you, Doctor Lewis."

"Likewise, Dr. Walker." He turned and entered the small door.

Major Cartwright waited until the door had sealed before speaking. "He's a good scientist. Very thorough, one of the best. If there's something there, he'll find it." he said, then hesitated for a moment. "His new assistant confuses me a little. I hope she's up to the task."

"She could just be nervous. She looks pretty young, and we were all unsure of ourselves at that age. Your uniform *is* intimidating," Anna said with a coy smile. She couldn't resist the temptation to take a jab at Cliff.

"That could well be," he said, as he watched Lucy and the computer support technician as they rushed down the hall, clipboard and cart of new computers in tow. He sighed. "I need to get back to overseeing the upgrades. I'll find you if there's news."

Anna nodded, and walked back in the direction of her office. Something didn't seem right about this whole situation. She needed more information. It was like a puzzle, and it demanded to be solved. She kept coming back to Lee's bright smile and warm eyes, and wondered how a man so cheerful could work with corpses all day.

Chapter 5

The news on the radio sounded grim, but Anna knew the situation was far worse. The riots had spread to cities neighboring the capital. Disturbances were being reported on buses and planes leaving the area. She wanted to work with the other researchers to contribute to a solution, but she was mired in paperwork, emails, and hourly interruptions from Lucy and Major Cartwright. She was desperate to be in the labs, running tests and analyzing the data, but she had many other tasks to prioritize first.

The first samples had been sent for analysis. The upgrades to the center provided by the military allowed them to test for drugs and toxins. The small local hospital did not have those facilities on hand, and transporting them to the nearest major hospital would have created unacceptable delays. It was late, well past the time she usually went home. She didn't like upheaval in her routine – she couldn't even keep track of Trisha's chaotic schedule. The words on the screen meshed together to form an intimidating wall of text. She blinked, forcing herself to concentrate. She promised herself – *just one more email before I leave.* There was always one more email.

A powerful knock suddenly hammered against the door. She recognized Major Cartwright's distinctive bang. "Come in," she said, as she contained an exasperated sigh.

"Sorry to disturb you. I wanted to let you know that most of my staff and I are heading out for the night. Need anything before we go?" The deep lines in his face enhanced his obvious exhaustion. He appeared to have aged ten years throughout the day.

"No, thank you. I was just putting the finishing touches to one last email." She was grateful for the news. She didn't have to feel guilty about going home now.

"There's always one more thing isn't there. Go get some rest. We'll be back at seven o'clock. A few are staying overnight to finish a few things." He ran a hand through his hair, his stiff crew cut was unaffected by the gesture.

"More like ten more, but I can do those from home."

"Your dedication is noted, but you should get some rest." He smirked.

"Okay, okay. You win. I'll see you at seven." She gave in, and stood up as she cleared her desk and picked up her cellphone. She felt more at ease with the major. Despite her reservations about the military in general, she found him honest and easy to work with.

"Good night." The major replied, and closed the door on his way out. Anna heard feminine giggles drifting down the hallway. The sound was alien and out of place in the grim new laboratory. She picked up her purse and left her office. The halls of the facility were deserted. She could hear fragments of conversations behind closed laboratory doors. A young military man, a private, nodded politely to her as she approached the entry door. She recognized him from earlier, his name was Bruce and he served as Major Cartwright's assistant. She opened the door and found herself bathed in a warm summer night.

The usually deserted picnic table was occupied. Heather sat alone, watching traffic. She rubbed her arms. Her face was drawn and pale. Anna was curious about the sullen young woman. "Hello, Heather."

The girl nodded. "Good evening Dr. Lewis." She spoke with an unfriendly, formal tone.

"Are you feeling alright? You look cold."

"Working in a morgue does that."

"Oh. Is there anything we can do to make you more comfortable?" It had never occurred to Anna that morgue work could be chilly.

"Not unless you have some beef jerky. I'm starving." The other woman maintained her standoffish attitude.

"Can't help you with that. Try a sweater."

Heather ignored Anna, and resumed staring at the highway.

Anna continued towards her car. She sensed something about Heather was wrong, but she had no idea what.

The drive home was uneventful. The radio reported riots and clashes in towns only few hours away. Anna hoped they could find something, and soon. The police were advising that everybody stay indoors if possible, and to avoid excursions into the affected areas. She shook her head. The situation seemed like something gleaned from a movie. Not reality. It was too horrible to be real.

Once home, she found the empty house disconcerted her. She felt haunted by the video she'd seen earlier. Turning on all the lights, she tried to settle into a good book. She was listless and she flipped through the pages, unable to relax. She wanted it to be morning, so she could get her teeth into the problem. She also wanted to get those bodies out of her cafeteria.

She went to bed, but she lay awake for a long time, staring at the shadows that wavered on the ceiling. Sleep came, spotted with nightmares of being pursued through a strange city, chased by a ravenous gang of bloody husks that screamed for blood.

Chapter 6

It was just before seven o'clock in the morning when Anna arrived at the facility. The parking lot was almost full. She pulled into her reserved spot, and was relieved that Heather wasn't sitting outside. She had been tempted to bring the strange woman a bag of beef jerky as a peace offering. This time, however, there were armed guards posted outside, and they demanded to see her identification. Once inside, she noticed a constant bustle of military men rushing between labs. The hallways had been cleared and restored to their former emptiness. The presence of strangers changed the ambiance, and contributed to the spooky emptiness of the moment. It felt as though she was entering the building for the first time. She made her way to her office, and forced herself to maintain a cheerful demeanor. Nobody needed to know how disturbed this project made her. She walked past the students' workroom, which had been converted into an office for Major Cartwright and his staff. The eclectic collection of posters and events still hung on the walls, untouched. Computers covered the small worktable in the center of the room. About ten army people were pressed shoulder-to-shoulder against each other, in a room that could hold five comfortably. Cliff wasn't there, but Bruce was. She passed on a message for Cliff, and she walked on towards the cafeteria.

Heather stood outside the morgue, scowl imprinted on her face. Her hair was disheveled, and her small glasses set crooked on her face. Heather's tightly drawn lips had a bluish tings and she stood, glaring at a stack of papers. Anna was determined to avoid her and didn't slow down.

"What is your problem?" She heard Heather's voice hiss behind her.

"Excuse me?" Anna turned to face the girl. She had tolerated enough rudeness.

"You're late, you didn't reply to any of *my* emails all night long and I had to work all night!" She shouted the words, wild-eyed, and her hands shook.

"I'm sorry you feel that way. Would you like to come to my office and talk?" Anna didn't want to have this argument in public, and was having difficulty maintaining her composure. A group of military personnel were already watching the spectacle. She took a step back.

"A lot of people are going to die, and it's all *your* fault!" Heather said, glaring. Her face became flushed and she bared her teeth at Anna.

The morgue door opened. Lee stepped out. "What's going on out here? Heather, I need you inside."

"Alright, fine." Heather shot Anna a poisonous look and marched back into the morgue.

"Nothing to see here, boys. Back to work." Lee said as he waved off the gawkers. They dispersed and silently returned to their posts.

Anna inhaled deeply. Her heart pounded, her face was hot, and her insides quivered. "Thank you, Lee."

"You're welcome. I've learned to give her a wide berth." He winked. Anna relaxed.

"I guess I'll talk to you later. It seems I have some emails to catch up on," She said as her face sagged. She could only imagine what kind of vitriol Heather had sent her.

"I've scheduled a meeting for eleven o'clock. I'm waiting for a few more test results."

"Anything interesting?" She wanted to calm the nagging voice in the back of her mind, the seed of doubt that Heather had cultivated.

"Yes, but I don't want to get into it prematurely. Suffice it to say that I've requested more specimens. Cliff is working on that as we speak." Lee said with a satisfied smile. Anna could barely contain a repulsed shudder.

"Well, let me know if you need something." Anna replied, trying to be diplomatic.

"I might drop by if there's time. I have a lot of samples to take, and even more to plan for."

"Okay, good luck with that." Anna said. Lee chuckled in reply and walked back into the morgue. Anna was glad she remembered to make peanut butter sandwiches for lunch.

Chapter 7

Anna pursed her lips as she sifted through her clogged inbox. Many of the emails were from Heather. Anna wasn't sure why she needed to receive these messages. They were self-aggrandizing, and contained very little information. She bragged about things as mundane as preparing tissue samples, or making microscope slides. Anna skimmed the rest and filed them in a folder she named 'Heather', in case of problems later on. She was uncertain about how to deal with the woman, because Heather's hostility wasn't based on any realistic complaint. Time dragged on. She wanted resolution – answers. She deliberately left the radio turned off. She didn't want to hear the news; she found it was too disturbing.

The door opened. The receptionist, Lucy, let herself in. She wore a deep necked blouse and dress pants in stark contrast to her usual casual attire. Her cheeks were rosy, but rather than a smile she wore a confused frown. Anna found Lucy out of place in the new, renovated research facility. She seemed alive and worldly, in stark contrast to the sterile labs and scientists. It wasn't an unpleasant observation, because it reminded Anna she was still alive.

"Just let yourself in. Closed doors are made to be opened." Anna said her voice was singed with dry humor. Lucy was incorrigible, she preferred to barge in unannounced.

"Don't be like that! We're friends, remember?" Lucy said, being characteristically boisterous and persistent. It seemed so surreal to Anna.

"Okay, what do you want?" As much as she enjoyed sessions of playful banter with Lucy, Anna wasn't in the mood.

"I wanted to make sure you're okay. I overheard some of what went on. I can't believe that bitch!" Anna wished Lucy had been discreet enough to close the door.

"I'm fine. The conversation was a little fucked up, you know?"

"Yeah, yeah. Well, you're not the only one." Lucy scandalously raised an eyebrow as she spoke.

"What do you mean?" Anna's curiosity was piqued, even if she wasn't one for gossip.

"I just bumped into her in the hall. She looked down my shirt and practically *snarled* at me." Lucy said while she giggled.

"Wow, that's just — wow. She's *so* jealous!" Anna couldn't help wondering if Heather was actually mentally ill.

"Yeah, and guess what happened last—" Lucy was interrupted by a rap at the door, which she had left partly ajar.

"Come in," Anna said.

Major Cartwright walked inside, and his smile melted when he saw Lucy. Awkwardness permeated the moment. "Um, I have to go. I have lots of papers to read. Work!" Lucy backed out of the room. Anna wanted somebody to tell her what was going on. She remembered when she ran the place. But, that was yesterday. Now she was relegated to pushing papers and herding scientists. She hated the bureaucracy that had been forced upon her.

"What can I do for you, Major Cliff?" She resisted the urge to laugh. The world was ending, and she was worried about Lucy and Heather.

"I just wanted to stop by and let you know that we've secured more specimens, and they're being moved into the morgue as we speak."

"Oh, more bodies. Just what the doctor ordered."

"Actually, yes." He paused for a moment, and continued, "Also, I've put in a request for a new assistant for Dr. Walker. It seems there are too many problems with Heather."

"I hadn't noticed," She said, allowing herself a small smile.

"We need people with level heads. This isn't a time for personal glory. We are a team." The major said, his voice conveying the strength of his conviction. Anna agreed with him.

"I'll leave that in your capable hands." Anna said, hoping he'd be able to fix the problem before Heather wanted to have another conversation.

"Excellent. I'll see you at the meeting." Cliff said, stepping out, and he pulled the door shut behind him.

Anna sighed, and tried to put the situation out of her head by burying herself in her work. Doctor Grant's team of graduate students had made good progress in maintaining his experiments. She'd heard nothing from

Doctor Evans, but her tests were expected to take hours to incubate. At least something was going as planned. The morning dragged on, and the eleven o'clock meeting loomed like a dark stain on the day.

Chapter 8

Anna found herself sitting in one of the annoying, squeaking chairs. She was afraid to move, because the noise embarrassed and distracted her. Lee was setting up the projector, as Major Cartwright took the seat across from her. The chair groaned under his weight, much to Anna's relief. Doctor Grant sat next to her, and Doctor Evans took a seat next to him. The chair next to Major Cartwright remained empty. Anna studied Lee as he struggled to make the screen readable. His face looked much paler, and his hands were shaking as he examined the plugs. He mumbled under his breath, and shook his head.

"Okay, so your projector doesn't like me. Right now we have our associate researchers in the labs sorting out these results. I think we're going to be busy for some time." Lee began. His voice was rough and he maintained a slow pace, as though the words were difficult to form. He paused to take a sip of water. "First, I should let you know what I did not find. This wave of violence doesn't seem to be caused by any drug or disease we can test for. That's where the good news ends." He looked at the table and drew a deep breath. This didn't seem like good news to Anna. Some new designed drug would incur a horrific toll on society, and would be as much work as a disease to treat.

"However, what I did find defies all medical explanation. I wish my slides worked, but I'll just have to rely on my own descriptions. There are multiple dissections left to do, but I felt some of this couldn't wait."

"What I found most striking were the variable decay rates. It's like parts of the body died hours, or even a day or more before the given time of death." Lee finished, and reached for his glass.

"How is that possible? Was there some kind of underlying condition common to all of these people?" Anna asked. It just didn't, couldn't, make sense.

"That's one of the more interesting mysteries. Well, they're all interesting, actually." He paused, and continued "It's almost like there were two times of death, and the rest of the tissue only figured it out after the individual got shot."

"What?" Major Cartwright interjected, fists clenched on the table.

"Muscles, digestion, nerve function seemed alive and well, give or take. Circulation, on the other hand, seems to have stopped, as did many other systems that were not needed for either locomotion or digestion." Lee explained.

"That's impossible!" Doctor Grant exclaimed, his face contorted with confusion.

"In normal circumstances, yes, I would agree with you." Lee said quickly, as if to derail one of Doctor Grant's diatribes.

"Have you come up with an explanation?" asked Doctor Evans, her quiet voice wavering.

"That would bring us to the second mystery. A lot of these systems have been modified. It's almost like I'm looking at cells that aren't human."

"Could it be an aftereffect of carrying that much necrotic tissue in the body?" Anna asked, fascinated by the implications. She was ready to pass off her administrative duties so she could dive into the science. She knew Lucy could cover most of her current duties in her sleep.

"No, this is like something invaded and rebuilt the cells for their own purposes. The samples are being studied as we speak, but it almost looks like the muscle tissue was reinforced."

Anna straightened; the abrupt motion caused her chair to make an audible squeak. That statement brought her back to the memories of the horrific videos and pictures that they were shown the day before. She could still see the impossible feat of quartering a fully armored combat soldier. She looked at Major Cartwright, who appeared to be deep in thought. "You know, yesterday, in one of the pictures, there was a soldier who was torn apart. They didn't even react to getting a beat-down from the police. Maybe that's how they seem impervious to injury?"

Major Cartwright nodded slowly. "Yes, that would be a good starting place. But, we have to know, is there a way to stop this and get our people back?" The major stared at Lee with an intense hawkish stare.

"I can only speculate about that for now. There are too many unknowns. The changes are so extensive that it might not be possible to cure the disease without killing the host. Their brains seemed fine, but we don't have the technology to deal with that kind of challenge."

"So, they're still aware?" Doctor Evans asked, her voice incredulous and subdued.

"Well, I'd need a living one to run tests on, but we really don't understand enough about the brain to know for sure," Lee offered.

"Okay then, so are there any other commonalities among the victims?" Anna asked.

"That's the funny thing. They're pretty diverse, and our sample size is admittedly small. But we did find, on most of them, a scratch or human bite mark. The others may not have had enough left of them to identify such a wound."

"If this is transmissible, then I need some options!" Cliff said, the anger rising in his voice.

"I'll find you some." Lee said, his voice conciliatory. He took another sip of water.

"If we can't reason with them, we need to neutralize the threat." The major was insistent.

"If all else fails, I suppose we can use fire." Lee looked at the floor while he made the suggestion.

"Explain." Cliff broadened his shoulders.

"Most every kind of protein will be permanently damaged at temperatures in excess of sixty degrees Celsius."

"And how does that help us, exactly?" Cliff's knuckles were white from holding his fists clenched for so long.

"It's like how you can't un-cook an egg, Major." Anna blurted out.

"So, if we burn them, then we stop whatever's changing them?" Cliff asked.

"That's the theory," Lee said, and continued: "But, their brains are fine. The people are possibly still in there!"

Doctor Evans gasped. "We can't burn them alive!"

"It's an option." Cliff said, his voice like cold iron.

"How could that ever be an option?" Anna said, but as she remembered the photograph of the burned bodies, she realized that it had already been an option.

"We've already used flamethrowers to prevent a barricaded elementary school from being overrun. It was a terrible decision, but the commander there had to buy time to get those kids out of danger. The sight of their burning companions did nothing to keep the bastards back." Cliff offered the new information through clenched teeth.

"Maybe there's some kind of receptor blocker that's keeping them from acting rationally?" Doctor Grant asked.

"I'm not a neurologist, but if this thing can completely change how the body works, that would probably be child's play to a bug like this." Lee took another sip of water, but his hands were visibly trembling.

"But what if they're still in there? They have rights!" Doctor Evans said. Her voice shook as she spoke.

Before anyone could reply, an agonizing scream echoed down the hallway. Anna jumped to her feet, as a cold chill ran down her spine. Cliff was the first to reach the door, and Anna pushed Doctor Grant out of the way as she ran outside. Doctor Evans remained frozen in her chair. Another scream twisted through the facility's halls. Anna felt herself running after Cliff towards the screams, when every fiber of her being urged her to run the other way. The cries were coming from the main entry. Anna hoped Lucy had a reason to be far away from her desk. Lucy was her best friend, along with Trisha, and she couldn't let her get hurt. The screams got louder as they ran, and more desperate. Men's shouts soon joined them.

When they rounded the corner, Anna stopped in amazement and terror. Doctor Grant crashed into her from behind. Anna broke her fall with her hands, and a sharp pain surged up her arm, but her eyes remained transfixed on the scene ahead. She could neither right herself, nor look away.

A young intern sat slumped by the door of the cafeteria, broken glasses on the floor next to him. His lab coat was torn open just below the neck. The expanding bloom of crimson blood clashed with the pristine white of the cotton. His left hand lay upon the wound, and his fingers trembled. His expression was blank, as his lips moved as though he were talking to himself. He shook and seemed oblivious to the scene as Heather attacked Lucy with an inhuman ferocity. Lucy was pinned to the ground and she struggled against her assailant, but her resistance did not deter the other woman. Blood pooled on the floor. Lucy cried out again as Heather tore flesh from an exposed breast, as Bruce, Major Cartwright's assistant, struggled to get a grip on Heather's shoulders. Judging from the bite marks on his strong arms, he had tried before – and failed. He flinched as a spray of blood hit him in the face. Lucy's arms fell to the ground, and her screams quieted to a pained moan.

"Lucy!" Anna screamed, her own pain forgotten. Doctor Grant and Cliff pulled her backwards, and hoisted her to her feet.

Lee pushed past them. "Heather! What the fuck wrong with you?"

Heather stopped mid-rend, her eyes focused on Lee. She snarled. It was animalistic, a sound no human should be able to make. Lucy twitched slightly. The color of her face was beyond pale. She fell silent. Heather straightened. Bruce capitalized on the strategic opening, and jumped, he used his shoulder to tackle Heather. He pinned her to the floor, forearm hard against her neck. "A little help!" he cried out as he dodged an attack from Heather's free arm. Men armed with guns stormed onto the scene, but were unable to find an opening to fire.

Anna rushed to Lucy's side. "Somebody call the hospital!" she cried as she pushed down on the gaping wound in Lucy's chest. The pain in her wrist was unbearable, but she ignored it. She had to save her friend. "Get me a first aid kit!" She didn't know first aid, but she knew enough to apply pressure. Lucy's eyes fluttered. "Come on, Lucy. I'm here, you're going to be okay."

Cliff knelt down and pulled off his jacket. "Get to a safe place, you don't need to see this," he said, elbowing her out of the way as he wadded up his jacket and pushed it against the wound.

Lucy's lips moved. No sound came out. "I'm not leaving her!" Anna shouted, her voice almost drowned out by Heather's howls. She took Lucy's pale hand in her blood-soaked ones, and held tight. Lucy's skin was cold, but Anna felt a slight tug from Lucy's icy fingers. "I'm here, Lucy," she said gently, then frantically to the people standing around: "Is an ambulance on the way?" she called out, her voice loud and frantic. Her concentration was broken as Heather's legs flailed and struck her in the small of her back. She flinched and angled her head to watch, hair sticking to the cold sweat on her face. The big man breathed heavily as he fought to hold Heather in place. The spray of blood on his face had begun to dry – lines of sweat drew the drops downwards across his face.

Major Cartwright turned to the man, his eyes wild. "Do whatever is necessary! Keep her contained!" he barked as he pushed the blood-soaked jacket down harder on Lucy's wound. Anna didn't know how much blood her poor friend had left. Cliff sighed, and turned back to Lucy. "Stay with me, Lucy. I'm sorry about what I said last night. I wasn't respectful. I shouldn't have called you that." Lucy's head wobbled from side to side. Her motions were unsteady and weak. Cliff continued whispering to her.

"Where's that damned ambulance?" Anna screamed. Heather's growls had lessened. Bruce, who had subdued

Heather, was crushing her windpipe. Her flailing attacks were more desperate, but less coordinated. The other men began their assault – raw and brutal – as they slammed the butts of their rifles into Heather's face. Anna didn't want to have to watch her die, especially now that she knew Heather had no choice in how she had behaved recently.

"I got through just now, I had to call a few times." Lee walked over, sliding his cellphone into his pocket. His eyes passed over the scene and he said "Holy shit," under his breath.

"What do you mean, you had to call a few times? It's 911!" Anna said.

"The lines were busy." Lee explained with a quiet voice. Anna realized if the chaos from the city had migrated here, their mostly volunteer town emergency services would be overwhelmed and untrained for a situation of this magnitude.

"So they're coming?" Anna asked.

"They said as soon as they could send somebody. Calls like this are coming in from all over."

"Do you realize what that means?" Anna asked, hoping somebody would contradict her.

"Yes. It's a disease, and it's spreading," Lee offered. "But I just don't get it."

Anna turned to face him. Out of the corner of her eye, she saw Heather's face. Her tongue was puffed and hung partially severed from her open mouth. Her face was unrecognizable, beaten into a mass of shattered bones and pulverized flesh. Her slight body spasmed and fought against Bruce's weight, and he worked to keep the pressure constant. "Don't get what?" She was nauseated. She had opted to study microbiology because she couldn't handle gore. Now, she was embroiled in a struggle for her best friend's life – while watching another woman being beaten and strangled to death. She took a deep, cleansing breath, though the blood scented air brought little relief.

"Well, most of the bodies had some kind of human-inflicted injury." Lee elaborated.

"Point?" Anna asked, angry that she needed clarification.

"We've never been around them while they're alive."

"So if it's an infection, how did she get it? And why are you okay?" Anna knew what this meant, and it wasn't good.

"We were exposed to bodies. It must have an airborne vector." His face fell as his voice trailed off.

"Wouldn't that mean you're infected, too?" Anna asked in a hushed tone, hoping Cliff wouldn't hear.

"I've spent most of my time away from the morgue, analyzing data. Heather did the dirty work." Lee admitted.

"You're feeling alright, Lee?" Major Cartwright interjected, looking up from Lucy's bloodless face. He had been listening.

"I feel fine. Just a little hungry." Lee replied, watching Heather's body convulse. Her movements slowed. "Strange how long it's taking to strangle and bludgeon her to death."

"How could you say that! It's horrible!" Anna could not accept how calm he was with the reality that his own assistant had succumbed to the enigmatic condition. Now he was observing how long it took her to die.

"Don't lose your objectivity. Yes, it's fucking horrible." he snapped, and took a deep breath to regain his composure. He continued: "But, we need to learn as much as we can." Lee drew the words out.

Anna sighed as she turned back to Lucy's body. Her friend was very still, and even paler than she had been before. She squeezed Lucy's cold hand. No response. "Oh my God, Lucy! Wake up!" She shook Lucy's arm her motions became violent and desperate. She couldn't bear the thought of losing her best friend. "Cliff, do something! Don't leave me Lucy, I need you. We still have to travel the world together and be like Thelma and Louise. Right? Right? Right?" She kept repeating that word, as though it would wash all the wrong away.

Cliff unwrapped is fingers from the blood-soaked jacket he was using to stem the flow of blood. His fingers searched along Lucy's throat for a pulse. He shook his head. "No..." he began, his voice faltering. Then he swallowed and continued "Lucy, I'm so sorry."

Anna loosened her grip on Lucy's hand. The blood had dried, gluing their hands together. Anna winced in pain as she unclasped her fingers. She suspected her wrist was broken. Her skin pulled as she moved her hands, as she placed Lucy's slender hand across her motionless stomach. Anna gazed at her friend's beautiful face and cried. She didn't hear the paramedics as they raced their gurneys down the hall. She didn't feel Cliff's arms around her. All she could perceive was the anguish of anger and loss.

Chapter 9

Anna stood mutely as the paramedics evaluated the intern's injuries. The young man shivered while being examined, his eyes vacant. He wouldn't answer the medic's questions; he would only stare into space, mumbling the "Stop," over and over again.

Major Cartwright and Bruce had left soon after the paramedics arrived. Cliff needed to make arrangements to keep the facility secure. Anna doubted any of them would feel safe for very long. She had helped Lee drag Lucy and Heather's bodies into the morgue to prevent decomposition and contamination. Anna held her breath the entire time she was in the cold, sterile room as she held the door open. She noticed that Lee did the same. Under normal circumstances, she would have found the validation of one of her quirks endearing, especially with respect to hygiene. Lee was talking on his cellphone, making arrangements for the bodies and samples to be moved to a facility better able to handle airborne pathogens.

Anna was feeling vulnerable and decided to give Trisha a call. She didn't know of a better way to learn about what was going on at the hospital. She also wanted to make sure her surviving friend was okay. She didn't like how it has taken so many attempts to reach the hospital and 911. She walked back to her office, but first stopped at the washrooms. She needed to wash her hands, even if it felt like she was washing Lucy away. She scrubbed and as the water in the sink became blood red, a single tear ran down her face. Her wrist throbbed with pain. She resolved to find some bandages after she had called Trisha. Her hands felt raw by the time she stopped. She dried her hands, made a quick dab at her eyes, and walked to her office.

Her cell sat on her desk. When she picked it up, she noticed she'd missed a call from Trisha, but there was no message. She redialed, and waited. Trisha didn't like voicemail, so the phone rang for a long time. Anna was about to give up when her roommate answered. "Hello?"

"Trisha! It's Anna." she said, trying to submerge the shakiness in her voice.

"Anna! Are you okay? All hell is breaking loose. I can't talk long."

"Here too. I'm okay, but Lucy isn't." Anna choked back a sob.

"Oh no! What happened?" Although Trisha had only met Lucy a few times, they had always gotten along well.

"She got attacked by one of those ... things ..., and we couldn't stop the bleeding. And—" her voice trailed off. She couldn't say the words.

"Oh God, not Lucy too. We've been flooded with this all day. It's like a nightmare." Trisha was quick to anger, and this was no exception.

"It can't be here!" Anna was in disbelief.

"People are eating each other and turning into animals!" Trisha said. She sounded so tired. Anna wondered if she was still on the same shift as last night.

"But how did it get here? It was just the capital." Anna said, perplexed and afriad.

"You know about this shit?"

"Well, kind of. We've been researching it." Anna didn't know what was and wasn't classified anymore, so she decided to be deliberately vague.

"Hurry it up, then! We're going to run out of beds. I have to go."

"Okay. Please stay safe." Anna said, not wanting to hang up.

"You too." Trisha hung up, and Anna was left with her thoughts. She needed more information. She turned on the radio and stared through the small window in the back of her office. The streets were mostly deserted. The park across the street seemed empty. Anna closed her eyes and leaned back in her chair. The news on the radio was intense and frightening. Over fifty confirmed cases of unprovoked attacks in her small town, and the numbers continued to rise. People were being advised to stay indoors. Anna didn't plan on leaving without taking along a guard or two. They were also being told to keep their blinds closed. She couldn't see the point in that, as her window faced a secluded park.

She sighed and stood up, knowing the time had come to attend to her injured wrist, and went to look for their first aid kit. She had no idea what had happened to the one in the cafeteria, so she decided to look for Lee to see if he knew. She wandered the halls while she cradled her hurt wrist in her good hand. She finally caught sight of Lee leaning against the door frame outside of Major Cartwright's makeshift office. Her shoes squeaked against the polished floors. Lee turned at the sound. "Anna, just who we needed to see. Are you okay?" Concern was etched in the lines of his face. He looked so old.

"Not really. I busted my wrist up and it's starting to swell. Any idea where I can find a first aid kit?" Anna asked.

"I have something, I was just patching up Bruce," Cliff answered. He seemed distant. He opened and slammed drawers until he pulled out a roll of bandages. "You want the honors, Lee?" he asked.

"Sure, I could do with working on a live one for a change." Anna shot him a poisonous look. "Come on, it was just a joke." He sighed as Cliff tossed him the bandages.

"Just get it over with," she said, almost growling. "I'm in no mood for your dark sense of humor."

Lee nodded, and she held out her wrist. He wrapped it tight. "That should do until we can get you checked out."

"Thanks. What did you need me for, again?" She didn't want to think about the hospital.

"We're evacuating, and soon. We want you and your staff to come with us." Major Cartwright spoke, his words chosen carefully. "They're on the move, and this location is indefensible. I just sent Bruce and most of the others out to build blockades out of whatever they can find to slow them down."

"What about the experiments, and cultures? We just can't throw those in a bag and run!"

"That was my point exactly," Lee said.

"Our people's lives are more important than samples. There are new samples walking all over the place now." Cliff said, shifting in his chair and his palms pressed against his desk.

"Great, so you want more cases like Heather." Anna couldn't accept that all their work had been for nothing, that Lucy had died for nothing.

"No, I didn't say that. Getting our samples out will take time we probably don't have."

"Do you want to stop this infection or not? How many more people need to die before you take a stand?" Anna said, unwilling to have allowed Lucy and Heather to have died for nothing.

Major Cartwright shot to his feet. "How could you even suggest that! I have ordered men to their deaths, do you think I would ignore their sacrifices?"

"Then let us finish our work!" Anna yelled, all of her composure melting away.

"Hey, hey! Calm down both of you" Lee came between them and waved his arms. "Come on. Cliff, you know our samples are important. Help us. You can get us the help we need to hold out while we get everything ready to go, and arrange for an airlift once we get to the base by road. It's not like they can stop a giant armored truck." Anna flexed her bandaged hand experimentally as Lee spoke.

"It would take some doing." Cliff's voice trailed off.

"It would be easy. I can get the researchers and interns packing. I'm sure we could get everything out. Any delays would put us back at square one." Anna interjected.

"This goes against all of my better judgment. As far as I know this is the first team to even begin work. Losing anybody here is not an option. The reports we send out can't replace your staff," Cliff said.

"A lot more people than that are going to lose if we can't find out how this thing works." Lee said as he fixed a hard gaze on Cliff. He continued: "It's airborne, we know this now."

"I'm willing to take the risk. These are people we're talking about, not just some grant money. We need to find the answer." Anna was surprised by how brave she sounded.

"Alright, I'll work some magic and get us some cold transport," Cliff relented, and as he sank back into his chair, and picked up his phone.

"By the way, Anna, where is Doctor Evans?" Lee asked as he whisked her out of the major's office. "Some of her tests should be finishing soon."

"I'm not sure, I haven't seen her since the meeting." It felt like an eternity had passed since then.

"Look her up, and I'll deal with Doctor Grant," he smirked as he spoke.

"Sure, I'll hunt her down." Anna said with a frown— she regretted her choice of words. Lee waved, and walked down a fork in the hall.

Chapter 10

Back in her office, Anna held the phone with her shoulder as she looked out her window into the deserted park. Doctor Evans hadn't answered the phone in her office, and the interns who worked for her hadn't seen her since morning. Anna left them with instructions to begin packing the samples and to cooperate with the other teams. Now, her last recourse was to try Doctor Evans' cellphone and home lines. Anna was perplexed – Doctor Evans wasn't the type to skip out on work, especially during an important project.

The call to the doctor's home line went to voicemail. Anna retrieved her phone and hunted through the contacts, all the while bemoaning her lack of personal organization skills. She was searching by last name, but couldn't remember if she listed Doctor Evans under her full name, or Frances, or Fran. Anna's peripheral vision caught sight of a figure approaching the park. She paused, and moved closer to the window. The figure had gray hair and was tiny. Anna realized it was Doctor Evans. But why was she outside?

The woman scurried across the street and rushed past the deserted bus stop all the while looking over her shoulder. Anna could make out another figure in the distance –moving with a fast, deadly grace. Anna froze as terror consumed her. It was going to happen again. The scene was muted by the thick windows in her office. She grabbed her phone and dialed Cliff.

"What can I do for you, Anna?"

"Oh my God Cliff, Doctor Evans is outside and she's being stalked by one of those things!" she shouted into the phone, all sense of moderation lost.

"Where is she?"

"I can see her from my office. Oh shit, she just tripped. Get somebody out to the park!" Anna gasped for breath. She could feel herself shaking. The monster was now very close to the fragile older woman.

Cliff barked instructions in the background, followed by distant, mumbled voices. "They're on their way."

It was too late. The creature – a tall, lanky man with black hair – leaped onto Frances' back. She fell face-first to the ground. Her hands clawed the turf in front of her mouth held open in a silent scream. The fiend drove its face into the nape of her neck. As it pulled away, a mouthful of flesh stretched and tore. Frances flailed and twisted, but was unable to free herself. Anna dropped the phone and began hammering on the glass, and screamed at the thing that only had the semblance of being human.

Time froze as the creature turned to face her. Its mouth was open wide and dripping with Doctor Evans' blood. A chunk of meat – of Frances – dropped onto Frances' still body. Suddenly, it bounded towards her window, its eyes fixed on Anna. Anna could only scream as it crashed into the window. Blood smeared across the glass as it cracked. She backed into her desk in her haste to get away. Again, it slammed its head against the glass. This time, it broke through. She screamed again and ran for the door. Her bandaged hand was useless with the simple mechanism of the door handle. An unearthly sound roared behind her, and panes of glass shattered on the floor just as the bolt released. She threw open the door as the monster hurled itself from the window frame towards her. She swung the door in its face, sealing it in her office. Then, she recoiled, propelling herself into the wall that faced her office door, where she cringed. Its screams paralyzed her with fear. It flung itself against the thin wooden door as it tried to break through. Anna was terrified. She didn't want to be eaten. She didn't want to be a monster. She dragged herself along the wall, away from her office door.

"Anna!" A deep voice called out. It was Cliff, but she was too afraid to look away from the door of her office. "Anna. We're here, it will be okay. The situation is under control."

Shots fired through her door. The creature's angry screams echoed down the hall. Anna slumped to the floor and pulled her knees to her chin. She trembled as tears ran down her face. "Doctor Evans—" she began, her voice cracking with a sob. The creature howled again. More shots were followed by a blessed surreal silence.

"I know. We were too late, I'm so sorry." Cliff said, stepping into her field of view.

"Why had she gone outside at all?" Anna said as anger shot through her.

"We don't know. I guess nobody ever will."

"This is all so horrible. These monsters. And they're still human! What the fuck?"

"We're doing everything we can. You know that." He placed his hand on her shoulder. She noticed he now carried a small gun. Despite its size, it gave her a measure of comfort.

"She died for nothing. Fucking zombies killed a woman who had a chance of finding a way to help them!" She hadn't used the term zombie before. No one had; zombies were imaginary, things concocted for scary movies ... but she realized now, maybe they were more than that.

"Is zombie going to be our official diagnosis?"

"Sure, why not. We have to call them something." A name was reassuring. It made it easier for her to accept the situation, and to create some emotional separation from the work.

Cliff chuckled, but his expression did not change. "Let's find Lee. The transports are arriving in a few hours, and we need to sort out this situation." He took her good hand and helped pull her to her feet. They walked away from her office. Neither turned to look back.

Chapter 11

Preparations didn't take long. Doctor Grant, in a rare act of benevolence, agreed to supervise Doctor Evans' team. Several of the post-doctorate students volunteered to continue her research and were set to familiarizing themselves with the various tests and findings. Fortunately, she had left her computer unlocked which allowed them to access her files without delays. Frances had been very well organized, a quality which improved their chances of continuing her work. Anna looked forward to her own more research-oriented position at the new facility. Cliff hadn't said much about the new location, just that it was remote and isolated.

Once the body had been removed from her office, Anna went to retrieve her personal items. They hadn't bothered to clean the floor in their haste, and had left a grotesque brownish pool of blood. The office reeked with the stench of decay. Her window had been covered by a simple tarp. Distant screams floated through the air along with the occasional peppering of gunfire. She jumped at every one. She discovered her cellphone had been immersed by the pool of blood, and left it there. She tried calling Trisha on her desk phone, but there was no reply. She left a message on their home phone line, just in case. She didn't want to be reported missing.

She met Cliff and Lee near the exit. Most of the staff and equipment had already been loaded onto another personnel carrier. Cliff joked that it wasn't luxurious, but it would get them to their flight safely. Armed guards surrounded the perimeter, and the shots grew more frequent and intense.

"You got everything?" Lee asked. Anna nodded and remained silent. She tried to appraise his features, to determine if he was infected or not. She couldn't tell. Deep voices trickled through the glass doors – voices deep and urgent. Primal shouts were followed by more spurts of gunfire.

"Okay, move as fast as you can. They're coming." Cliff ordered.

They ran out the door. The large green vehicle idled in front of them, at the curb. Anna heard a series of howls behind them. She turned, to see a pair of blood-soaked zombies had broken through the barrier and were rushing towards them. Two soldiers lay prone on the ground. Their group sprinted for the carrier. Anna's ankle twisted under her, and she tumbled to her knees. "Cliff!"

Cliff ran towards her and drew his gun. Anna recognized one of the monsters. It was Bruce. He grabbed her bandaged arm, and his icy grip was so strong; she could not pull away. Cliff aimed behind her. She closed her eyes and held her breath. He fired twice. Then Bruce's grip on her arm fell away. "Come on!" he shouted as he hauled her to her feet. Lee had made it to the vehicle, and held the door open. Anna stumbled towards him, half being dragged by Cliff. Her ankle throbbed, but it could still bear some weight.

Anna gasped for air as she climbed in. She sat down next to an army man she didn't recognize. He nodded to her politely. The door slammed shut and the truck began to move.

Anna remained silent for much of the trip. The vehicle rocked back and forth. She felt motion sick and raw. Cliff and Lee whispered to each other. Some of the students talked quietly amongst each other, while other clung to papers and sat motionless, staring into space. She tried to calm her mind. Her close call had been so terrifying that she continued to tremble. Today, she had lost two friends.

It was unfathomable. She didn't know how she could adjust to that kind of trauma. She couldn't forget Lucy's terror or Doctor Evans' inexplicable and ill-fated walk in the park.

They arrived at their destination, after spending hours on the long, hot road. After a brief pit stop they were loaded into a small plane. Anna only noticed two small engines on the wings, and the cramped interior made the personnel carrier feel spacious. Cliff told them they would need to stop to refuel, but it would take them almost a day to reach their final destination. Anna was dismayed that they had such a long distance to travel in so small a plane, but Cliff explained that the larger planes had been diverted to humanitarian relief.

Once on the plane, Anna remained awake as the others fell asleep. It was late evening, and she was feeling restless and cold. Her hand throbbed – and the bandaging was too tight. She loosened them, being careful not to disturb the wrist itself. There hadn't been time to see the medics at the base before leaving. She was also starved and wished there had time to eat. The field rations were disgusting. She wasn't sure what they were supposed to imitate, but it wasn't food. She'd bravely made the attempt, but she had found herself unable to manage more than a few bites without feeling nauseous.

She scrutinized her injured arm, and her heart dropped. Two small gouges lay just under the edge of the bandages. "Damn it!" she muttered under her breath. It was a death sentence. Then the panic took hold. A part of her was convinced it was just shock, which sleep would clear up. But objectively, she knew that wasn't the case. She estimated that she had a few hours left. Then, she would be one of them. She would kill all these people in the cabin with her now.

She pondered the alternatives. They still didn't even know what this disease was. There was no logical hope of containment. Tears began to run down Anna's face. She couldn't see any other option.

Her mind processed the new information, another piece of this terrible reality. Before, she had so much to live for. Now, something irreversible was happening to her. She had come to respect and admire Cliff and Lee. And she couldn't fathom injuring the students, who had their entire lives ahead of them.

Anna watched Cliff across the aisle. He still had his gun. She could end it, and keep her friends safe. Even without her, they might eventually find a cure. Her mood was tinged with bitterness. She wasn't yet forty years old!

It was clear that Cliff was in a deep slumber. Anna decided she would take his gun and then shoot herself before they could stop her. The engine roared as they flew. If everybody really was asleep, then they wouldn't be aware of anything until she pulled the trigger.

Anna crept over. Her hands trembled, and suddenly she found herself unable to fully control them. Remembering how Heather had begun shaking uncontrollably for hours before she transformed, she became certain the shakes were a part of the disease's progression. It was hard to call them zombies—she was on the fast track to becoming one now! Her good hand worked to undo the safeguards. Cliff was still fast asleep. Anna dreaded the next phase of her plan.

She slid the gun free.

She'd watched people shoot themselves in movies, but this was real. She wanted to minimize the mess, and feel as little pain as possible which meant she had to get it right the first time. The pistol was small; she figured sticking it in her mouth would be the most efficient way to go about it. Anna didn't know for sure.

She placed the barrel in her mouth and closed her eyes. The cold steel clattered against her teeth. The taste of steel danced on her tongue. She flipped off the safety. She knew what she had to do. It was her duty to her friends. She wanted to stop this thing – whatever it was – not add to the misery.

"Anna! No!" Cliff shouted. She felt his hands on the gun. The barrel slipped out of place. Her broken wrist shot intense pain down her arm as she fought Cliff. He was a strong man, but his powerful arms had trouble controlling her. Then, a pair of hands were on her shoulders, pulling her backwards.

"No, I have to!" she cried out. "I'm infected!"

"No, anything but this." It was Lee's voice behind her.

"Stop me now, this is the only chance you'll get!" She pulled forward, knocking Lee off balance. She had become much stronger, but still in control. Her muscles ached from the exertion.

When barrel came into view, Anna pulled the trigger.

Blinding pain seared through her face as the bullet grazed her cheek, then ricocheted and left a window shattered. Anna's ears rang from the intensity of the noise and the sudden pressure change popped her ears. Cliff snatched the gun, while Lee dragged her back into a seat and examined the wound. "No –" she began, but trailed off.

"That's enough out of you," Lee said, then he paused and a sick smile crept across his face. "I need to find a way to secure you. Seems you're going to help with our research one way or another." Lee said. Wind howled through the window. Stray papers flew across the small cabin. Some of the students were crying, other cowered in their seats. Anna sighed and looked out the broken window. She thought she saw smoke.

"The pilot should have some handcuffs. I'll go check." Cliff said, snatching papers from the air along the way to the front of the plane. The papers crumbled, his knuckles turned white from the intensity of his grip.

The plane lurched. Cliff stumbled forwards, hitting his head on the door to the cabin.

Then a voice crackled over the speaker. "Fasten your seat belts, an engine is down and we have to land. Remain calm." Students screamed, and Lee rushed to Cliff's side.

The pain and chaos was too much for Anna. But just as exhaustion overwhelmed her and she blacked out, she heard a panicked cry from the front of the plane.

"Fire!"

Zombie Bedtime Stories, part 3

Deadlocked

Prologue

Frank Leblanc watched in silence as his partner Haley walked to her house. He was a stone-faced man of about fifty years, slim and much taller than average. His light brown hair was flecked with grey, and deep frown lines ran through his face, while crow's feet obscured his blue eyes. He seldom had reason to smile. The attack on Haley earlier that day had rattled him; the idea of being attacked by a friend in cold blood would disturb anyone; even on a good day. Since it was his birthday—his definition of a bad day—the assault had left him seething with anger. Haley was a good kid; she reminded him so much of his own daughter, Kelsey.

Kelsey. Several years had passed since she died, back in 2030. The doctors still didn't know how to treat the rare genetic disease that had sent her down the path to a slow and painful death. He shook his head, forcing the memories from his mind. Kelsey was gone, and his wife had left him for another man: he was alone. Frank pulled away from the curb once he saw that Haley was safely inside. She was so like his Kelsey. They were both warmhearted and caring, empathetic to a fault. They were the polar opposite of him. He decided to deal with the problem the only way he knew how—work.

Chapter 1

Frank was pissed off. Some jerk had taken his assigned parking spot. He didn't recognize the car, so he parked his beat up sedan—the pride of 2027—in the first available guest parking spot. He had contemplated trading it in for a fully-electric model, but he had reservations about being dependent on the strained local power grid. He'd enjoyed gloating when the early-adopters had become stranded during the nuclear crisis years ago. Even now, the memories of their sheepish smiles and sputtering disbelief made him chuckle. He slammed the car door shut, and hardened his face into its usual stony countenance. As he walked to the station, he noticed how full the parking lot was.

He strode in the front door, and allowed the door to slam shut. The station was deserted—reading tablets were scattered across tables and abandoned cups of coffee grew cold. He'd returned with the hope of finding an available person that he could partner with in order to get back to work and forget about the whole incident. Of course he'd have to deal with the annoyance of working with somebody he wasn't used to, but it was better than no work at all.

"There you are, you old bastard." Frank turned towards the voice, which was quiet and raspy. The man that stood there was his supervisor, and he delighted in antagonizing Frank. Gerald was a squat little man with greasy thinning blond hair and he was growing a terrible attempt at a goatee. They had been partners years ago, but their mutual disdain was all that remained of their formerly good working relationship.

"You were expecting the tooth fairy, maybe?" Frank said.

"You took long enough, Leblanc. I don't remember you driving me home anytime I got hurt." The bitterness seeped through Gerald's voice. An on-the-job accident had relegated Gerald to clerical duties three years ago, and he remained resentful to this day.

"I didn't want you in my car!" Frank spat out.

"Maybe if you bothered to get a girlfriend, you could have your own daughter to taxi around. Or, is there something else you want out of her?" Gerald said, smirking during the insinuation.

"Leave the kid out of this, Gerald. I assume you want to talk about work?" Frank said, hoping he wouldn't need to work with the man ever again. He ignored the suggestive goading, but a part of him wanted to send Gerald thumping down a flight of stairs.

"Yeah. I need you to work the retirement homes. Everybody else needed to be sent out on emergency calls."

"Do I get a partner?"

"Did you hear what I just said? We have nobody else; you're on your own. I'll send you the list, and we're pulling out some old ambulances from storage. Take one when they arrive." Gerald turned then and marched out of the room. Frank glared at the light reflecting off the shiny bald spot on the back of the man's head as he left.

Frank sighed as he took a seat with a view of the glass doors, so he could see when his ambulance would arrive. He didn't look forward to being relegated to ferrying old people to their tests and medical appointments. His anger at Gerald stewed inside him. *What a presumptuous little pig!* Frank thought. He had never told Gerald about Kelsey. He wouldn't have understood, even when they had been partners. Frank knew it was best to suffer alone. Working with Haley was a painful mixture of therapeutic and depressing. In a way, it was like having his little girl back. Like Haley, Kelsey had also befriended the homeless and taken care of local children. Kelsey had always wanted to be a doctor, while Haley was saving to put herself through nursing school. He suspected they would have been great friends, if Kelsey hadn't... it was always so hard to finish that thought. He remembered how pale Kelsey had become, skin translucent over a body that could barely move, before her hair fell out. Frank's eyes were brimming with tears, so he stood up and paced around the room.

He hoped Haley would come back to work soon.

Chapter 2

It was late afternoon by the time Frank managed to take a short break. Most of the teams that worked transports had been re-assigned to emergency response. Since he didn't have a partner, he was one of the few left to ferry long-term residents from their nursing home to their tests and doctor's appointments. He was relieved to be nearing the end of his shift, because he never knew what to say to people who were that old and sick. Thinking about incurable diseases or endless tests made Frank uncomfortable. He wanted to save lives, rather than observe the protracted death-throes of the terminally ill.

He pulled the ancient diesel-powered ambulance up to his next stop. He was a few minutes early, so he took a moment to close his eyes and relax. Cars passed by; the quiet and calm seemed surreal to Frank. Usually, Haley would be chattering about some charity event, gardening or whatever the humanitarian outrage of the week was. As always, the silence brought out his demons—the nagging doubts that inhabited his subconscious. He blamed himself for what happened back in the park. He should have been more vigilant, and pushed Haley out of the way. He should have done something, anything.

He fought against the feelings of guilt and regret. There was nothing he could have done. He'd been distracted, watching another hurt teen slink away from the scene. Poor kid must not have been insured, a common problem. He'd stopped trying to force treatment on runners a long time ago. There were free clinics in the city; if victims could walk, they could go there. There was no point in causing bankruptcy and more misery. The world already had enough poverty.

His thoughts wandered to the subject of the abnormally high number of emergency calls. Something didn't feel right about it. They were usually kept fairly busy—the city's crime rate made sure of that. Frank figured the anomaly was too sustained to be one large incident. Perhaps it could be explained by a number of freak accidents. That would be normal enough for a warm June afternoon, right when high school and college final exams were finishing. Coupled with a gang fight or two, that would be enough to tax their response rate, especially after yet another funding cut.

He was relieved that his last patient was an elderly man who not only appeared to be fast asleep, but also didn't need to be returned from the hospital. With the gurney secured, Frank began the thirty-minute trip through the inner city. It was a gray, treeless place that teemed with urban life. Its inhabitants roamed through the concrete jungle, oblivious to the out of place, antiquated ambulance. He approached Calypso Park; once lauded as an achievement in inner city beautification, its trees had since died of neglect and vandalism, while rare tufts of crabgrass graced the once seeded, manicured grounds. He could see a group of figures gathered by a trash can. As he drove past, Frank caught a glimpse of a mob swarming a pair of individuals fighting on the ground, trying to pull them apart. It was a typical day in the park. He was glad his shift was over; somebody else would have to deal with the aftermath.

Once he finally arrived at the hospital, he was surprised by the number of ambulances that were waiting to unload. He idled and waited for them to clear. He observed the casualties with detached interest. First, there was an overweight middle-aged man lying quietly as they rolled him in. Next, were a small child of about seven, and her mother. Both had bandages bound around their forearms—crimson blood spotted through. The mother held a piece of gauze against her daughter's throat, but the tide of blood had violated the chaste floral print of the girl's sundress. Both stared into space, the child shaking in her mother's arms, neither making a sound. Frank remembered the fair-haired girl from the park earlier that day, the one Haley had tried to comfort before being attacked herself. It was the same eerie blank stare. He remembered how withdrawn Haley herself had become after the attack. It has to just be a bizarre coincidence.

More casualties paraded by. All were bandaged; many trembled and clutched still-bleeding injuries as they were wheeled into the hospital. Frank wasn't sure it was a coincidence after all.

Chapter 3

After what seemed like an eternity, Frank unloaded his patient. The man had never woken up throughout the entire drive, and a nurse confided that she wasn't sure where they would put him, given the influx of patients. *That's her problem*, Frank thought. However, he took his time in the hospital, and made a discreet round of the waiting room and triage areas. He saw that many people were covered in scratches, and had bandaged their oozing wounds with anything that could be found to bind them. One big man sat with a pair of khaki pants mashed into an injury on his arm.

As Frank continued to wander the hospital, the narrow corridors crowded in towards him. There was always a hint of claustrophobia when he visited these places. He attempted to smother the panic by trying to overhear pieces of conversations. The consensus seemed to be that most of the injuries were caused by random violence. People were attacking each other with their bare hands. Such brutality wasn't uncommon in this part of the city. The staff preferred to attribute the wave of violence to the full moon. Any other time, Frank would have found that analysis quaint and misguided. However, he had seen an attack up close, and he remembered how the Taser hadn't affected Buddy at all during their struggle. To Frank, it was becoming clear that this more than simple lunacy.

He turned one corner, then another. The walls were lined with makeshift beds; not unusual in itself, the hospital was decades old and at the limits of what expansion and temporary buildings could do to alleviate the problem. Most of the patients sat or lay down on their beds, with a barely-touched meal next to them. Most of the meat had been picked away, leaving the rest to be discarded. A small minority had cleaned their plates. They shivered, despite the almost oppressive heat and humidity. The cooling system had failed early in the summer, and the administration had yet to allocate the funds to repair it.

Frank stopped in mid-step. He recognized somebody. It was the fair-haired teenage girl from the park. She sat upright on her cot, and leaned slumped against the wall. She was rubbing her trembling hands together vigorously, as though she were desperately trying to keep warm. Her eyes were closed; they looked like dark, sunken pits gouged into her pale face. She was bandaged around the neck and shoulders, but spots of crimson marred the sterile dressings. Frank took a step backwards: the walls seemed to be closing in on him again. He had to get out, to breathe fresh air and get away from this chaos. He knew in his gut, that something was terribly, terribly wrong. He looked for a doctor on his way out, but he didn't see any. The nurse at the station evaded his questions, leaving him with an uncomfortable mystery.

"We're taking care of them. That's all you need to worry about," she told him. She was a large woman, who had caked on too much makeup over her tanned skin.

"They don't look right!" Frank retorted, growing angry. Why couldn't she see the obvious?

"Nobody who gets attacked looks right!" She said, as her flabby jowls shook with her words.

"Just check on them, please," he said, feeling defeated and ineffectual.

"Look, you bring them, we take care of them. So get back to bringing them in!" she said, turning back to her work.

Frank left the hospital dejected. There was nothing else for him to do but go home, and think.

Chapter 4

It was a long night. Frank found himself tossing and turning, unable to stay asleep for long. Every instinct told him something was wrong. The compulsion to run away and leave town was overwhelming. He paced around his one-bedroom apartment. Few decorations hung on the walls, and the white paint was marred by streaks of brown cigarette tar from a former tenant dripping through. Sometimes, the effect prompted Frank to imagine that his walls were bleeding. Dusty, wooden furniture was the main focus of the room; outdated and mismatched styles were predominant, much like with everything else he owned. No thought had been put into how the apartment was arranged, and the layout looked to have been designed by a child. The chaos suited Frank. He was never home; he preferred being at work, or visiting with the police. An aging television was mounted on the wall. It didn't receive any of the more advanced, interactive channels, but he could watch the few public broadcasts that survived. Frank eased himself into a worn out armchair. The back was split open and a flow of yellowed stuffing puffed out, but Frank found that the defect only augmented the chair's back support.

He switched to the morning news and found that all that was being covered were the typical mindless feel-good stories. A clip flashed by about a large number of fights overnight, and that residents were advised to stay away from the Calypso Park district. Also interesting was the announcement that the nearby hospital was above maximum capacity, and residents were advised to choose an alternative hospital for emergency services. Frank was relieved—riots weren't uncommon anymore, and more violence was to be expected throughout the next few days. He was worried about taking calls downtown, but that was part of the job; the police would be there if something dangerous was going on.

He turned off the television and made himself some toast for breakfast. He decided he'd spend the first part of his day hanging out at the local police station. They would have a better idea of how dangerous it was downtown and it would give him a welcome distraction from the events of the previous day. At least it wasn't his birthday anymore.

Chapter 5

The police station's parking lot was packed, though there were few police cars to be seen. Frank found himself jostled by two large officers on his way in. He didn't recognize them, which was also strange. The suburb he lived in was serviced by a small police station, and their small force didn't see many new faces. He saw his friend Marvin, a man in his early forties, working at the front desk. The man's uniform was rumpled in clear violation of protocol, and his curly brown hair was in a frizzled state of disarray. His strong features were bathed in the light of the computer monitor he was squinting at. He did not look like his usual, cheerful self.

"Hey, Marv. What's up?" Frank asked, keeping it casual. Usually Marvin was very forthcoming with information, especially all the juicy details.

"Frank? What are you doing here?" Marvin asked, as he straightened and looked up from the screen.

"Jeez, I just popped by to say hello. What got your panties in a twist?" he said. Marvin's attitude was confusing; usually he welcomed any opportunity to procrastinate and dissemble.

"Sorry, sorry," Marvin said, sighing. He continued: "We just have something going on. It's pretty big."

"Riots?" Frank asked.

"That's all I can tell you," Marvin said, while cutting off Frank's next sentence before it started.

"So, you're holding out on me?" Frank said, annoyed. He tried to take a discreet glance at the screen, but was hampered by Marvin's poor posture.

"Guess so. Shouldn't you be working or something?" the other man said.

"I go in this afternoon." He knew he was always the last to be called, even in an emergency. Gerald would ensure that he never qualified for overtime. Frank knew Gerald would never forgive him for his perceived role in the accident that landed him a lifetime desk job.

"You'll find out then," Marvin said, making his despondence evident. His phone rang, and he turned to answer it. "Wait outside; I'll come out for a break."

Frank stepped out the door without a word. The situation disturbed him. Everything was so peaceful, and quiet. Across the street lay a park, similar to the one Haley had been attacked in yesterday, but without a nearby school to populate the playground with throngs of children. A few families milled about the equipment. It was a pleasant sight, especially when compared to Calypso Park. Frank found himself smiling as he watched the children play. He remembered happier times, and sighed. Those days were long gone.

In a moment of weakness, he pulled out his cellphone. It was an older model, dented and chipped. Frank didn't care; it just needed to work. He was so anxious that he decided to call Haley to reassure himself that she was on the mend. Her cellphone went straight to voice mail. He decided to try her home line; he might get her boyfriend, and he might even get lucky and that goon would tell him something useful. Again, there was no reply. Haley's cheerful voice chirped their phone message through the small speaker. Frank left a short message, asking if she was feeling alright. Somehow, he suspected she wouldn't be. It was that gut paternal instinct, the same feeling that had told him that Kelsey's aches and pains were more than simple fatigue and the stress of being a college freshman.

"You got called in to work?" Marvin asked, startling him. Frank hadn't realized that Marvin was standing behind him.

"No, no. Just checking on a friend," Frank said.

"I didn't realize you had friends, Leblanc. Other than me, of course," Marvin said, smirking. They'd known each other since high school. Marvin had been the youngest brother of one of Frank's friends. They had reconnected when Frank moved back to the city shortly after Kelsey's death. Marvin's older brother had been killed by a drunk driver soon after high school, a tragedy that had prompted Marvin to enter the police force.

"Just a coworker, really," Frank replied.

"You can do better than that. Is it a girl?" Marvin was an incorrigible matchmaker—Frank had lost count of the number of times Marvin had tried to set him up with some nice girl.

"Mind your own damn business, Marv."

"Okay, okay. I'm just looking out for you. You're alone too much," Marvin said.

Frank couldn't help wondering if he wasn't alone enough. "Shut the fuck up and tell me what's going on out there," Frank insisted, wanting to change the subject.

"You didn't hear it from me. Deal?" Marvin said in a hushed tone, his Adam's apple straining as he waited for Frank's acknowledgement. Frank nodded, and Marvin continued: "Okay, so there's been a lot of fights around, but these ones are different than the normal gang fights and assaults. We can't reason with the assailants. We can barely apprehend them."

Frank couldn't believe what he was hearing. "So there really aren't any riots or gang fights, like on the news?" he asked.

"That's just to keep people from panicking. We're not sure what's going on," Marvin admitted, gazing down at his feet.

"When did it start?"

"Early yesterday morning, as far as I'm aware," Marvin said.

"Fuck, I think one of them attacked my partner yesterday." Frank was livid, and he felt betrayed. Why hadn't anyone warned them? This was something first responders needed to know!

"Are you sure?" Marvin said, incredulous.

"Skinny homeless guy that took four responders to get him off her, and he didn't even feel a damn Taser! That fucking thing worked, trust me."

"Shit, that's not good." Marvin's voice dropped. He paused, and then continued: "Is that who you were calling?"

"Yes." Frank couldn't manage any other words. His old anxieties were forcing their way back into his mind, and he just stared at the cell phone he was holding.

"Damn, I'm sorry. I'm so sorry."

"What? She'll get better. I just don't want another rookie to break in." Frank was good at misrepresenting his compassion as selfishness.

"We can hope."

"And just what do you mean by that?" Frank asked.

"Nothing, I'm sure it's nothing. If she was well enough to go home, she'll probably be okay." Marvin rushed through the words.

"What about the ones that don't go home?" Frank remembered that blond girl from the park, her face drawn and pale in the glare of the hospital's florescent lights. *She* did not seem to be recovering normally.

"You'd have to ask a doctor. I just know there are lots of casualties." Marvin wouldn't make eye contact; his gaze seemed to be drawn to the ground, far away from the laughter of the playing children in the park.

"I'm going to go check on her. It was good talking to you," Frank said, as he turned to leave.

"Wait!" Marvin shouted as he grabbed Frank's arm. His grip was tight. He continued: "Where does she live?"

"What does that matter? She's in Sunnyside."

"Damn it! Don't go." Marvin tightened his grip.

"Why the fuck not?" Frank asked. He was tired of Marvin's word games.

"We've lost some patrols down there. It's ugly."

"So we've gone from just some fights to losing patrols of trained, armed men? I gotta get her out of there!" Frank exclaimed as he tore his arm from Marvin's grip. He could still protect Haley.

"Those things are attacking everyone. It's not safe!" Marvin said, desperation seeping into his voice. He continued, pleading: "Don't go. Just don't."

"So what am I supposed to do? Sit around and let my partner get torn to shreds?"

"I can try to get you into a supervisor's car. They're checking the patrols out fairly regularly," Marvin said, rushing through his words. He paused, and then added: "It might take some time, but as a friend, I'm not letting you go out there alone."

"I don't care how I get out there, Marv, I just want to save my friend."

"Hold that thought for when my ass needs bailing out," Marvin said, and took a moment to lick his drawn lips. "Now, come in and have a seat. I'll get you fixed up."

Frank nodded and looked out at the play equipment once more before following Marvin into the building. He wanted to get moving, but Frank didn't consider himself a hero, and wasn't keen on placing himself in harm's way.

Chapter 6

Frank had dialed Haley's numbers twice more before Marvin emerged from behind the reception desk, but his signal appeared to be failing. There was still no answer, if the number dialed at all. His anxiety threatened to overwhelm him. He looked up, but his friend's expression was totally unreadable.

"Okay, it took some doing. You owe me," Marvin said.

"Much appreciated. When do we leave?" Frank asked. He was afraid it was already too late.

"You know Del, right? He'll be taking you in a special car we've started using. It keeps you hidden from those things."

"We'll go to Haley's?" Frank said as he nodded, but, he didn't know Del very well.

"That took some extra convincing. Now, follow me."

Frank stood up and followed Marvin into the back. He'd never been in the restricted parts of the station before. White walls and omnipresent fluorescent lights washed out every surface. The doors leading to many small offices lined the walls. Officers rushed up and down the hall, jostling Frank and Marvin as they walked. Screams echoed down an adjoining hall. There was no coherence or language to them, and they were relentless. "Don't worry, they're locked up and we're not going that way," Marvin said, and they continued through the station. Frank noticed small beads of sweat forming on his friend's brow as they continued through the building. Marvin opened a door at the end of the hall, and they stepped into a small garage. The door blocked out the screaming when it closed, a small mercy. A group of mechanics was hastily moving their tools out of the way of a parked police car. The vehicle's windows had been tinted completely black.

"Is that even legal?" Frank asked.

"We're the police," was Marvin's pointed reply. A man walked up to them and Frank immediately recognized him as Del. He was tall with a slight build, and he had a big head with a long, thin nose gave him a comical bird-like appearance. He had shaved his head since the last time Frank had met him, and it gleamed under the harsh artificial lights, making Del look like a bronze statue of some forgotten ancient God. *The God of Baldness maybe*, Frank thought, allowing himself an inward smile.

"Frank! Good to see you again," Del said as he

extended a hand to Frank. His facial expression didn't show any hint of pleasure, rather, it held an expression more akin to exasperation.

"Likewise." Frank accepted the handshake. Del's grip was strong, in contrast to his thin arms.

"You're in the back. Piss me off or get in my way and you're walking back," Del said as he opened the driver's door. Frank was relieved that the tinted windows would hide him. He didn't want to have to spend years deflecting attention from the pictures that Marvin would be sure to take of him in such a compromising position.

Frank silently moved to the rear door. He checked to make sure Marvin wasn't paying attention, opened the door and slid inside. A sheet of bullet-proof clear metal separated him from the front seats. His long legs pressed against the protective barrier, forcing him to shift in his seat to find a bearable position. Frank figured he was going to be late for work, but he didn't care anymore. Gerald could go to Hell.

They left the station's garage and drove into deserted streets. The playground stood empty. Del explained that everyone was being told to stay indoors and not to interact with strangers, and to notify the police of strange behavior.

Any other day, Frank would have presumed that the warnings were simply a defensive measure against a litigation-happy population. However, today it seemed like these announcements actually had the best interests of the population, rather than those of the city, at heart. A dark smear on the sidewalk caught Frank's eye. Because of the tinted windows, he couldn't tell if it was just a spill, or blood. Goosebumps danced over his skin, despite the stuffiness of the poorly ventilated car.

Frank wanted to know why they needed to check on the patrol cars in the area, but he'd been told not to ask questions or piss off Del. He still wasn't sure why Marvin had been insistent that he not come out here alone. The streets were empty, and other than that suspicious stain on the sidewalk, things seemed as normal as circumstances would allow; Sunnyside was a pretty standard suburb, boring in all the right ways.

"First stop. This won't take long," Del said, before flipping a switch on the dashboard. The clear metal instantly went dark, as did the windows. Frank could hear the blood rushing through his ears, countering any rumors of silence being deafening. He'd heard about this new feature in modern police cars, but he had never expected to find himself in the back seat of a cruiser to see it firsthand. It was designed to pacify aggressive criminals, or to prevent sensitive police information from being overheard. Inside its confines, the outside world seemed not to exist. As the moments ticked by, Frank found his anxiety levels rising. His knees pressed painfully against the clear metal barrier, while the dim halogen light at the top of the car's roof cast a murky glow over the backseat of the car. It was a claustrophobe's nightmare. Frank forced his breathing to remain steady. In any other situation, he'd consider installing these windows in his own apartment. However, his apartment was much roomier than a police car, and a lot less intimidating. This reminded him of times he'd been locked inside closets by his older cousin when he was small. Sometimes, he'd been trapped for hours. Except now he was bigger, an adult, and he couldn't even yell for help. Minutes dragged by. Shadows cast by the small light bulb seemed to twist in on themselves, contorting into new shapes. The sound of his pulse seemed deafening as it raced through his awareness.

The windows lightened then, blinding Frank. A rush of sounds dazzled his senses and seemed to intermingle with the flashes of light. Even the air smelled lighter and fresher. Sirens echoed in the distance. He began to relax, while trying to make it seem like nothing had been wrong in the first place. He made a mental note to never accept rides from cops, at least not in their special cars. Del was sitting up front, keys in the ignition. "A little warning would have been nice, you know," Frank said.

"Sorry, but I'd have to shoot you if you listened in," came the aloof reply. Del's voice was subdued. He started the car. Frank sighed. He knew there'd be many dark, caged stops for him before they finally reached his destination.

Chapter 7

It was mid-afternoon. Frank had noted many more suspicious stains on the pavement, but kept his theories to himself. Del had grown more withdrawn with every stop. Frank didn't want to push the man; that might result in spending the rest of the trip in the dark or walking, which was probably worse for his long-term wellbeing. The back seat was bad enough without near-total sensory deprivation. He wondered if it could be construed as cruel and unusual punishment. Unfortunately, few people would speak up for criminals—Frank himself was surprised that he was sympathizing with them. His eye caught a flicker of movement down a distant street—it looked like an army truck, but he wasn't sure. After so much time in the dark, he didn't trust his own senses. The wailing of sirens was almost omnipresent now, twisting down the soulless suburban streets. Frank noted that their route through the suburbs had circled the border to downtown. He didn't get why the radios didn't work, that would be much easier than visiting each stop personally. Even a cell phone would do the trick.

"Okay. Sunnyside coming up," Del said.

"About time. Why can't you just use a damn radio anyways?" Frank asked, feeling perilously close to the end of his rope. He checked his phone, but he had no signal in the shielded car.

"Too many interfering signals. And the cell network seems to be overloaded—I tried before I left," Del replied. Frank wondered what could cause such widespread interference. The network had been overhauled with new antennas to allow for very heavy usage in an emergency. Del continued: "Also, I have to make sure they're not asleep on the job."

"I thought they cleared the interference problem up five years ago, during the power crisis," Frank said.

"The damn army decided otherwise." Nobody had mentioned the army before.

"Here? Already? They took a fucking week to get here last time." Frank's interest was piqued; the military was seldom involved in civil strife.

"Some army bastard has his goons scouring the city, and ordered us to stay out of their way. Meanwhile, we're low on manpower as it is and could really use some help keeping this mess contained." Del had begun to rant, and

Frank decided to let him continue.

"That's kind of odd." Frank wanted more, but he was afraid of what he'd hear.

"I mean, we can barely keep those goons out of Sunnyside! The power is out in parts of the city and nobody answers the damned phone at the other stations. Fuck!" Del growled the words, his knuckles turning white has he clasped the steering wheel. They turned onto Haley's street. The trees swayed in the wind. Nothing else moved.

"What do you mean—" Frank began, but was cut off.

"Oh shit!" Del slammed the brakes, lurching Frank forward into the metal barrier. Crushing pain shot through his kneecaps. The seatbelt caught his chest before his face connected with the clear metal. Frank growled under his breath.

"Missed the damn stop sign again?" Frank was not amused, and Del's driving left much to be desired.

"No, we're here. Fuck. Stay in the car," Del said. He drew the words out, and his eyes transfixed on something just beyond Frank's field of vision. Del's head and a still-blooming lilac bush obscured the view.

"I have to see Haley," Frank said as he struggled with

his seatbelt. He tried to see past Del's tall profile, but could not.

"She's not there. We need to get out of here."

"How do you know that? Let me out!" Frank pounded his open palm against the barrier. He could feel old fears surfacing, the same ones he'd endured throughout countless surgeries with Kelsey.

Del sighed and the car crawled forward. Frank noticed the man kept a hand hovering over the blackout button. Frank doubted it was anything he hadn't seen before. After decades in the service, he figured he'd seen everything. In fact, Haley's shock and horror at some of their calls was an endless source of amusement for him. Frank looked out at Haley's yard, where he had dropped her off less than twenty-four hours ago. Another strange stain crept down the sidewalk by her front gate. As they moved closer, one of the newly familiar stains had crept to a mangled body that lay discarded on the green grass.

Frank's eyes widened and he assessed the scene, allowing his honed instincts to analyze the situation. White hair crowned a face that had been stripped to the bone, and the grinning skull gazed towards the sky, eyes still wide open. Frank noted that very little exposed flesh remained.

It was like the old woman had been eaten by wild animals, but, he knew this one was different. There were no scattered entrails. All of the attack had focused on exposed flesh and muscles. Frank's attention snapped back to why he was really here: Haley.

"She's in trouble! We need to get inside!" he shouted, knowing the monster that did this could still be lurking nearby.

"Looks like something already beat us to it," Del said flatly, nodding towards the front of the house. The glass in the sliding patio door was shattered. Blood smeared across the remnants of glass that remained intact. Smoke spiraled out the gaping hole.

"Del, let me out. We can help her!"

Del sighed. "No. It's too risky. These things attack people. Any people. They don't care who you are, or if you give a damn. Why do you think I drive this tinted car?"

"But what can we do?" Frank wouldn't accept defeat. Not this time.

"Fuck it. Go if you want to. I'll give you two minutes. If you hear screams, run back to the car."

Frank nodded as he heard the curbside door unlock. He shuffled his butt towards the door. Fear coursed down his spine and coalesced in his stomach. He wasn't a hero. He wasn't even sure why he was doing this, risking his own life. He should be at work, or better yet, hiding at home. When he swung the door open, his nostrils were assaulted by an intense bouquet of burning plastic mixed with the unmistakable reek of coagulating blood. He forced himself to ignore the corpse as he lumbered, stiff-legged, towards the shattered door. He noticed the sharp edges of the glass, and the human hair clinging to them. It was long, brown hair—Haley's hair. A wall of heat hit his face as he stuck his head through the hole to look inside, and the smoke spiraling out of the hole in the door stung his eyes and nose. The kitchen was on fire.

"Haley!" he shouted through the opening. He wanted to go in, but there was nowhere for him to go except the burning kitchen. Frank could hear the pop and sizzle of something roasting inside. The air had taken on the distinct smell of cooking meat. He wasn't a fireman, but the place gave him a bad feeling, and made him nauseous. "Haley, it's Frank! Are you still in there?" he tried again as he examined the hair on the glass. If she had escaped, why would she have thrown herself through the glass? It made no sense. He heard a car horn behind him, so he turned began to walk back to the car, head held low.

The car horn sounded again, twice this time. "I'm coming!" He heard a blood-curdling shriek then, and looking up, he saw a disheveled figure standing across the street. It was a tall man, dressed in boxer shorts and a bloody t-shirt. Frank froze for a moment, and then ran towards the car as Del hit the horn again. "Shit!" he screamed, as the bloody man began to charge towards him. Frank crashed against the door in his haste, and had just lunged into the back seat when the creature was upon him.

"Oh fuck! Frank!" Del screamed, and floored the gas pedal. Frank tried desperately to close the door, but the monster clung to the seat with inhuman strength.

Frank dodged a swipe from the man's filthy hand, cringing at the sight of the torn fingernails encrusted with dried blood. "We're not losing him!" he cried out to Del. Del immediately made a sharp right turn, and the creature was pulled away from the door. Frank slammed it shut and pushed himself into the far side of the car. His hands shook and he couldn't catch his breath. Was that the creature that attacked Haley's house?

Del brought the car to a stop after a few blocks. "I told you two minutes, Frank!"

"I don't think she was in there. Her hair was on the glass. She's somewhere out here!"

"So you want us to spend all day dodging these psychos so you can find your damn partner?" Del said through the glass.

"No, I guess we can't," Frank said, relenting to the harsh truth that he really had no idea how to proceed.

"Back to the station. I've had enough of Sunnyside." Del put the car back into drive and they pulled out of the suburban street.

Frank sighed. He could draw too many disturbing parallels between what just happened and the events of the previous day. He knew nobody would listen to him, though. He was just a paramedic, not a cop or doctor. Worst of all, he could only see the problem, and there was not a glimpse of a solution on the horizon.

Chapter 8

"Shit," Del said under his breath, a couple of blocks from the station. They'd spent the past twenty minutes sitting in silence, taking abrupt turns to avoid wandering groups of the possessed. Frank didn't want to talk. He was nursing the guilt of not being able to help one of his few friends. *Friend.* He'd never thought of Haley like that before. Usually, he thought of her as an exuberant annoyance.

"What now?" Frank asked, not bothering to conceal his irritation.

"More of those bastards, twelve o'clock," Del said, his voice hard with tension. The quivering anxiety returned to his stomach. Were they still safe inside the special police car?

With a grunt, Frank straightened his torso towards the steel-glass wall, craning his neck around the front seat's headrest. He could see two figures in the distance, walking in the same direction they were driving in. One was tall, and hobbled as he walked. The other had long brown hair and appeared to be wearing pink pajamas. There was a wrongness to their gait, a lack of purpose; this coupled with walking in the middle of the road, made Frank uneasy. "Can you go around them?" Frank asked. He didn't want another confrontation, and though he knew it was unbreakable, he didn't want to rely on the transparent steel barrier as his only insurance.

"The station is five minutes away. I have room to get by."

Frank didn't like it, but he enjoyed blackout time even less. As they edged towards the strange couple, Frank found that his hands were trembling. He clasped them tightly to soothe the nervous tremors. He wished there was something he could do, but it seemed to him that the time to act had long passed. He had all but given up on solving the mystery of what had become of Haley, but his eyes scanned the front yards of the houses they passed, looking for any sign of her. He knew she was out there, hurt and alone.

His gaze returned to the wretched pair walking down the center of the road. He found his eyes drawn to the woman. He noticed something staining the pajamas she was wearing—it looked like the brown crust of dried blood. Frank could only imagine what kind of coercion would compel normal people to become vicious and aggressive. He knew there were bad and violent people out there, but the average person was fairly docile and mostly harmless. She looked familiar, somehow, and Frank wondered if perhaps he'd met her at the hospital after one of his calls. He could see the outline of a lean frame beneath her sleepwear, and her long hair was a mess of matted tangles. A gaping slash ran down the back of her forearm. It hadn't been tended; the edges of the wound were splayed open, exposing white bone. Her scalp was coated with gore and blood. Frank was taken aback—no human could or should be functional in that condition!

"Pull up next to them, Del. She's hurt bad!" Frank said, concerned about the girl's condition. No matter how jaded he'd become, he still believed life was precious.

"This is the last time I take you anywhere, Frankie," Del said, exasperation clear in his voice.

Frank peered through the side window, to get a better look. "Oh, shit," he said as recognition rushed through his senses.

"What?" Del asked, peeved.

"It's her. Haley." Frank had only just realized it was her. She always wore her hair up at work, and he had no reason

147

to know what kind of pajamas she preferred.

"That's her? Fuck, man," Del said, shaking his head. They came to a stop.

Frank's eyes stung as he gazed at the vision of what remained of the vibrant girl he had known. She didn't seem aware of their presence and continued her silent march with her newer, equally-shocking partner. He observed deep cuts all along her scalp and forehead. His stomach lurched as the stains from her blood-soaked face spilled down her clothes.

"Is she one of them?" Frank asked. He hoped against all of his instincts that there was a cure, that they could scoop her up and medicate her back to some semblance of normalcy. The pharmaceutical companies had potions that could work wonders on a psyche.

"Yeah, I'd say she is," Del said with a sigh, then he paused and continued, "I'm sorry, Frankie. Our jail is full of them. We can't help her."

"I should have watched out for her. Done something when that guy in the park charged her," Frank said. The world seemed so much emptier. It wasn't fair, just like when he lost his Kelsey.

"This wasn't your fault. I don't know whose it is, but it

wasn't you," Del said in a half-whisper as he pulled away.

In despair, Frank looked back until the ghoulish pair were left in the distance. His throat was tight, constricting under the force of his distress. How could he move on, much less save himself?

Chapter 9

The police station sat in the distance, surrounded by a cluster of improperly parked police cars. Some had even encroached on the park across the street, which remained deserted. Frank was relieved that his own vehicle was not boxed in. He wasn't sure where he was going, but it would be far away from Sunnyside and the rest of the city. Frank felt queasy and shaken following his encounter with Haley. He'd seen many gruesome deaths, and even more grotesque injuries, but nothing could compare to the emptiness of her gaze, and her blood-encrusted countenance. He was angry at the twisted force that could compel a soul as gentle as hers to join those insane, craven fiends, but he knew she was lost to him, and humanity.

"I see remedial parking training is in order," Del observed aloud, as he navigated through the maze.

"As if they'd spend money on *that* when you need to expand that jail of yours," Frank retorted, in spite of his depression. He dreaded breaking in a new rookie. Gerald took a perverse joy in assigning him the happy ones.

"I'll make sure to keep a cell open for you next time

you decide to drop by," Del said, easing the car to a halt. He continued: "If there is a next time, I suppose. You get out of here."

"Don't have to tell me twice," Frank growled as he opened the door. He made a mental calculation of how far his car was, and slid out of the rear seat. He felt a sound in the air, a noise too distant to actually be heard, yet one that hung there, omnipresent in the air, like the scream of a dog whistle. When he slammed the car door, the bizarre sensation of sound was drowned out, but only for a moment.

"Help me!" a weak voice cried. Frank spun towards the police station, and the voice, wondering if his befuddled mind was playing tricks on him. But no, it was Marvin calling out to them as he pulled himself from behind the shrubs in front of the station. He clasped his gun tightly, his arm clawed against his chest like a misshapen wing. His other arm was mangled to the point of uselessness; strips of flesh had been torn from his forearm and the limb dangled loosely at his the side. Globules of slick blood trickled from his fingertips.

"Marvin, what happened?" Del asked. Frank was in shock, overwhelmed at seeing his only other real friend in such a horrific state. He was frozen in place, staring at that one limp arm, at the sharp tips of broken white bone poking through the gore.

"They wouldn't stop," Marvin wheezed, moving towards them. His gait was irregular, and he stumbled a couple of times before he reached them.

"Who? Who did this to you?" Del asked, reaching for his own gun.

"Everybody," was the shaky reply. Agony was etched on the man's face.

"You mean the prisoners escaped?" Del asked, his voice incredulous.

"No, everybody else. They changed. Why did they change?" Marvin replied, his body beginning to shake.

Everybody. That word chilled Frank to the bone. When they'd left, all had been under control. Now it seemed that officers had entered, and never left. "We need a first aid kit, Del!" Frank said. He wasn't going to accept that there was no hope for Marvin. He had to get him stabilized, and worry about whatever was spreading inside the police station later. Could it be a disease, some kind of virus?

"Check the trunk. Hurry!"

Frank wasted no time and rushed to the trunk of Del's

police cruiser, and found a Spartan box with few necessities inside. "Is this all you have?"

"Yeah, can't have your ass out of a job now can we?" Del said as he walked towards Marvin.

Frank made a quick inventory of the kit. Its quality was laughable, like something you might bring on a one-night camping trip. Most of the stuff was for superficial wounds, not bone-deep gouges. He grabbed the single roll of gauze and closed the trunk, hard, to vent his frustrations at the lunacy of the situation. He walked towards Del and Marvin, who stood together on the grass by the sidewalk. Marvin had grown quiet, and was shaking in the hot sun. Frank looked past him, to the doors of the police station. They were intact and closed, for now. "Okay, stay calm Marvin, let me have a look."

Marvin stared through Frank as he moved to examine the torn, mangled arm. Frank switched to a professional perspective. He didn't want to think about how his childhood friend had been mauled by those crazed things that Haley had become. As Frank examined the wounds, Marvin mumbled "Why?" over and over again. He needed immediate treatment at a hospital if they were going to save that arm.

Turning to Del, Frank said "We need to get him to a hospital." There was no other way; he doubted they'd be able to get an ambulance with all that was going on.

"How are we going to get him there?" With no radio, the phone system overwhelmed and the streets filled with rabidly insatiable people something as simple as a trip to the hospital became a very difficult proposition. Another haunting question emerged from the back of Frank's mind—how long did Marvin have until he became one of them? There was no way Haley would have voluntarily doused herself in blood and caused such gruesome deaths, and if she couldn't control what had happened to her, how could Marvin?

"That's a real problem," Frank said, mulling over the possibilities.

"Yeah, you don't say. We have to decide, and soon. I don't want to get torn to shreds once one of those things figures out how a door works." Del crossed his arms over his broad chest. Marvin appeared not to hear them; he seemed fixated on some point in the distance. There was nothing there.

"My post isn't too far from here. If you guys can hide in that fancy car of yours, I can try calling for an ambulance and get Marvin to the hospital. Even if emergency is full, I can keep the bleeding controlled."

"That's not exactly ideal," Del said.

"You got a better idea? We're wasting time. Those things that did this to Marvin could get out, and soon. We don't even know what's keeping them in." He paused for a moment, and before Del could reply he continued: "He needs a doctor... and then we need to get the fuck out of this city."

"You better hurry, then. I'll get him into the car."

Frank jogged towards his own vehicle, glancing backwards to make sure Del and Marvin had made it into the car. He needed some time alone. Everything that happened today had been too much for him to digest. He couldn't imagine a worse birthday. His consciousness flooded with regrets, both about things he'd said, or left unsaid, to Haley and Marvin. He'd never been a particularly good friend. Neither of those relationships seemed to have mattered, until now ... now that Haley was gone, and Marvin was likely to follow.

He climbed into his old car, started it and left the police station far behind. All he needed to do was procure an ambulance, and then he and Del could make their escape, which was probably easier said than done.

Chapter 10

The streets were quiet as Frank pulled up to the station. He considered himself fortunate that he hadn't encountered any of the possessed masses en route. Without tinted windows, he was a very visible target. He checked his mirrors, frantic for any early warning against approaching fiends. He didn't know what to call them. Usually you could talk to people, and although sometimes reasoning was out of the question, you could coerce them into stopping their attack. This anomaly that was happening around him went against everything he understood about humanity, even the negative parts. There *had* to be some element of self-preservation at play, yet these creatures appeared to have no compunctions against self-injury, leaping into moving cars with zealous abandon. He also didn't want to comprehend their unwillingness to tend to their own wounds, or replace soiled clothing, because the implications were disturbing.

He pulled into the parking lot. He was expecting it to be full, but it was eerily deserted. He spotted his prize—one of the old-style diesel-powered ambulances. Finding diesel was not difficult, and the vehicle had enough supplies to carry himself and Del out of the city and beyond the chaos. They might even find rescuers, a safe haven and some semblance of normalcy.

After parking his car, he dug up his trusty tire-iron from under the seat. It was heavy and cold in his hand. He gripped it tight, feeling the strength of the steel against his skin. He wasn't going down without a fight. There wasn't much else of value in his car, but still he felt a pang of sadness as he left it behind. He scolded himself for being worried about the car at all, especially after what had happened to Haley and Marvin. He marched inside, checking first to make sure the way was clear.

Once inside, he began the hunt for keys. The modern electric ambulances simply wouldn't do; if the power grid was down, he'd be marooned. He wanted the single diesel model that was still out in the lot. It was very quiet inside. His footsteps echoed as he walked through the silent building. It was as though every person who worked there had picked up their possessions and left. He wondered how many of them had fled, or worse, had become part of the enemy ranks. He found a few sets of keys still hanging on a hook at the back of the building. He scanned the hand-written vehicle numbers on the tags. All were for the newer models. The sense of urgency rose. He couldn't afford to linger here, and he couldn't see himself surviving without that ambulance. He told Del that he'd come back for him, and that's exactly what he intended to do. He began to brush aside papers and equipment, scattering the debris on the floor. The key had to be there, somewhere. Other than Gerald's office, there wasn't anywhere else where it could be, and his was the only door that was closed.

Frank was startled as his right foot hit something and sent it skidding across the floor. It was another set of keys. He rushed after them, scooping them up in his free hand. He almost laughed when he saw it was the right set! He could escape. He had never stolen anything is his life, but now he had no choice. His stomach churned with a mixture of fear and excitement.

He pocketed the keys and rushed to the door. He opened it and felt the hot June air smash up against his skin. He checked for the monsters. There were none to be seen, for the moment. A palpable aura of helplessness and panic seemed to permeate the outside world. Frank knew they could attack at any time, from anywhere.

As he was about to release the door, an angry voice resounded through the hall behind him: "You asshole! Just what the fuck do you think you're doing?" Frank spun inside to see Gerald's pudgy form advancing towards him. "You skip work, and then you come sneaking in here and don't even ask what's going on? You're going to tell me what you're up to right now, you son of a bitch," he finished as he breached the gap between them.

"I need that old ambulance to save my friend at the police station; he got attacked by one of those *things* and he desperately needs help." Frank hoped that his nemesis would show some humanity for a change. He owed the man an explanation for taking the ambulance; Gerald was his boss, after all.

"You didn't help me when I needed you, you selfish sack of shit. You got me put on desk duty when I needed a friend." Gerald spat the words out, his chubby face becoming red behind his blond goatee.

"Jesus, Gerald. How many times do I need to say it was an accident?" Frank moved to walk away, but Gerald caught him by the arm and held him fast.

"You collapsed that gurney on purpose, don't deny it. I lost my job and my entire life because of that," Gerald allowed the old resentment to rear its ugly head once again.

Enraged, Frank retorted: "I wish I had, because now I'd be helping somebody who deserves it." It was no secret that Gerald gave him the worst assignments and the most inexperienced partners, on purpose. He struggled against Gerald's grip; now was not the time for yet another pissing match.

Gerald shoved him, hard. The unanticipated assault caught him off-balance, and he stumbled out into the entryway. The tire-iron clattered to the ground. "What the Hell are you doing?" Frank asked. Screaming howls were audible in the distance. *They* were coming.

"You're not taking any ambulance from here, and when this is over, you're going to jail where you belong!" Gerald roared as he charged at Frank, taking a swing at his head. Frank ducked, and Gerald's fist grazed his left ear. He didn't want to hurt Gerald, and in truth the gurney incident had been a freak accident. Frank scuttled backwards a few steps, to maintain some distance. But, this was no time for a fight. They couldn't stay there; the monsters with human bodies were approaching, and they were hungry.

"Don't be a fool! You know those things are coming. It's not safe out here," Frank said, no longer attempting to mask the urgency and fear in his voice. He knew they were exposed to the danger, naked to its viciousness and spontaneity.

"What, your friends? I bet you're one of them, you backstabbing son of a bitch," Gerald said, and a sick smile came over his face as he continued "I bet you let your partner get attacked, used her like a human shield." Gerald's smile was malicious, he seemed to revel in the chaos of the situation, like the small, petty man he was. Frank could hear the howls and screams drawing closer. He didn't have time for this kind of insanity.

"We have to go!" Frank shouted in Gerald's flushed face. He could see something moving in his peripheral vision. A glance confirmed that the monsters, or zombies, or whatever they were, approached with an infernal grace. Again, he was the prey.

"No!" Gerald screamed as he flung himself at Frank. Frank side-stepped the attack, his heart pounded in his chest and threatened to jump out of his open, gasping mouth. Panic set in. On impulse, he skirted around Gerald's bulky form to reclaim his tire-iron. The fiends closed in. One among them locked his empty eyes onto Frank's own desperate ones for a moment. Frank gripped the tire-iron, and took a deep breath.

He whacked the weapon hard against the back of Gerald's head. The other man stumbled to the ground, and Frank took the opening to run towards the parked ambulance. The creatures howled as they converged on their newest prey—Gerald. Gerald's screams joined the cacophony as Frank made it to the vehicle and fumbled with the keys. His hands shook, and the panic of the situation and the horror of leaving somebody to that kind of death—even somebody who hated him—was threatening to overwhelmed him. He looked back towards the station. Gerald was still moving, or appeared to be. Frank couldn't tell if he was conscious and weak, or if the movements were a result of the cannibals feasting on his flesh. At last, he untangled the keys and bounded into the ambulance. He started it and gunned it like a madman towards the police station.

Chapter 11

The situation was much the same when he arrived at the police station. Guilt tormented him; he was a murderer. As much as he wanted to convince himself it was self-defense, he couldn't help but wondering if he could have done something differently and somehow saved them both. Frank didn't relish the idea of escaping the city with Gerald, but it was preferable to killing him. He wanted to wake up and have recent events be nothing more than a zombie-movie inspired nightmare, and start another shift being irritated by Haley's cheerful demeanor. The thought comforted him, so he indulged the fantasy a little longer. She'd tell him about her neighbor, or whatever volunteer work she was involved it, or about that hobo, Buddy. He'd tell her the world was gone to crap and everybody realized it but her. Frank sighed. As bad as things were in the world before, nothing could have compared to this.

He brought the ambulance to a stop at the edge of the chaotic mess of cars outside the police station; there wasn't room to proceed any further. It had about half of a tank of diesel; he'd need to find a way to refuel soon, and acquire extra supplies. That was secondary to his concern of getting Del and Marvin out, alive.

He looked around before disembarking, waiting to see if Del and Marvin would notice his presence and send some kind of signal. He checked his mirrors and opened the window a small crack. He held his breath as he listened for voices, screams or pleas for help. All he could discern was the rustling of leaves. No sirens or car engines could be heard. It was like he was alone in the world.

After a few moments of anxious procrastination, Frank decided to approach the police car. He slid out of the seat, leaving his keys in the ignition and leaving the door open. He'd learned the enemy was not interested in equipment. Only people.

He half ran and half tiptoed over to Del's police car. His heart was pounding, and he tried to push his earlier encounter with Gerald out of his mind. He waved at his reflection in the black tinted windows. He couldn't see what was going on inside. He looked around. The unexplained delay made him uneasy. He rapped on the window, hoping that the sound could be heard inside. While he waited, he glanced around the scene. Everything seemed tranquil enough.

Suddenly, the car began to rock. Frank took a step backwards, confused, by the unexpected movement. The car rocked again, and Frank watched as a crack began to form in the unbreakable glass of the driver's side window.

Impossible, he thought.

A hand erupted through the black glass, and then the crown of a head, pulverized and oozing blood. It was Marvin's head. Frank froze. It was unfathomable that these things could break through unbreakable glass, but he was seeing the proof, now, here, with his own eyes and left it left him feeling even more at a disadvantage. Marvin's other hand, mangled and shredded, now fought through the glass. A sickening sound of exposed bone grinding against glass grated the air. Frank shuddered as he watched the frightening facsimile of his old friend try to force his way through the through the car's armor. He couldn't imagine what kind of pain Marvin was feeling, if he could still feel pain. The idea of an individual's consciousness suspended in their bodies after the transformation was terrifying, and sickening. Frank could no longer stomach the horror, fear and despair. He screamed and made a desperate run for the ambulance. There was no way he was going to become one of them!

Marvin howled, and his voice distorted into something feral and savage. Frank could only imagine that Del was dead, yet another casualty of his own misplaced desire to do the right thing. He ran faster, and a glance over his shoulder confirmed that Marvin was almost free of the window. His friend's blood had spattered over the spotless white of the cruiser door. He was living a nightmare.

Frank grabbed the open door of the ambulance and swung himself around. In a single motion, he heaved himself into the driver's seat and slammed the door. He gasped for breath as he admonished himself for not exercising enough. At least he had a defibrillator handy.

He looked out the window and rushed to insert the key and turn the ignition. Marvin had freed himself, and was now charging towards the ambulance. His injuries and massive blood loss did not seem to impede his ability to use his arms. He was gaining, and Frank knew that he had no tinted windows to hide behind.

Frank put the vehicle in reverse and hit the gas. He realized he couldn't escape the city by driving in reverse, but he couldn't turn around without risking himself.

"I'm so sorry, Marvin," Frank said as he shifted to drive, and floored the gas. The ambulance charged into action, connecting with Marvin's body with a sickening thud. Frank felt the lurch as the tires rolled over his friend. His eyes stung with tears, and he turned around to examine his friend's remains. Marvin laid still, limbs strewn at unnatural angles. Frank fought down the urge to linger, to say something meaningful and profound over his dead friend.

He had to leave town. He wasn't sure where to go, but west, to the mountains, was as good a direction as any.

He needed to be alone. Worse still, he was a murderer... and now he was on the run.

Chapter 12

Frank kept his head low as he raced down deserted streets, trying to avoid being seen or identified. He wasn't going to let those things find him, or give them an easy meal if they did. His teeth ground together as he thought back on the day's events, until the pressure caused his jaw to ache. He seethed in silence, despite wanting to scream and hunt down whoever was responsible for this suffering. He didn't want to believe it was some type of freak natural occurrence; it was preferable to think of the infestation as a horrific travesty of justice. He swerved to avoid a pair of cars that had collided and had left parts of their jumbled wrecks strewn across the road. Broken glass crunched under his tires, while helicopters flew in the distant skies over downtown. Frank fantasized they were ferrying people away, to a place of safety, far from the carnage, with tall concrete walls topped with armed soldiers. He hoped the monsters couldn't get through concrete.

A passerby caught his eye, a bloody man waving his arms by the side of the road. Frank avoided eye contact and accelerated past the man. Nobody else was safe, at least nobody who looked blood-stained or wounded. After what had happened at the police station, he knew even being close to them was enough to spread the disease. He wasn't going to take any more chances, especially when the bloody man could turn into one of those things at any time.

Frank continued to brood about Marvin, Haley and Gerald. Haley and Marvin were his friends, and despite his antagonism, he and Gerald had also been friends at one time. The sounds of helicopters grew closer; he appeared to be right under their flight path. They were heading north, towards the air base that lay about an hour's drive away. The sound of occasional gunfire peppered through the air. It made Frank nervous, because if he could hear it, the people pulling those triggers were close. A crazed gunman could be every bit as dangerous as a zombie. The word was far-removed from the rigors of real life; zombies were fantastical monsters from movies and literature. However, the word zombie conformed to his new reality, and he could no longer discount the use of the word as inaccurate.

He sped by a stopped military vehicle, left abandoned across the left lane of the highway. It looked like a cross between a cold storage room and a personnel carrier. He'd never seen anything like it before, but wasn't feeling brave enough to investigate. He accelerated the ambulance to speeds that even *he* considered reckless. Whatever was going on there, he wanted no part of it, especially if it meant contact with *them*.

Frank could see the city limits in the distance, the looming sign and distant trees welcoming and alive. He was so close to escape, at least the part he could plan. A horn blasted behind him, and a quick check in the mirrors showed a small military caravan, and a roof mounted gun pointed directly at him. The driver was signaling him to pull over, so he slowed and pulled over on an overpass, where an attack could only come from two directions rather than any number of alleys or side streets. He took one last look at the city limits. So close.

A man wearing grey camouflage approached him. He carried a heavy gun, and his face was obscured by a cap. He barked some orders, gesturing towards the on-ramp of the overpass. Other uniformed soldiers disembarked from the vehicle and formed what could be considered a perimeter. Frank hung his head and unrolled the window. Maybe he could convince them to let him go. Screams echoed from below the overpass and the smell of smoke tainted the air. The monsters were close by—why were they stopped here?

The man marched up to the open window. He was young, with hard silver eyes. "Where are you going, sir?" He formed the words with deliberate intensity.

"I'm responding to an emergency. I need to keep going," Frank said, trying to keep his voice as flat and professional as he could. It was the truth, in a way.

"The local emergency networks have been down for hours. You're trying to escape town, aren't you?"

"This is an emergency situation. Why are you detaining me?" Frank said.

"I have orders from Captain McIntyre to prevent all infected from leaving the city. If you were a real paramedic, you'd know that." Gunfire peppered through the air, and accented the screams of the fast-approaching throng.

"I am a real paramedic, damn it. Do you think they just give these things away?" Frank remembered hearing Del talk about the army, and how some bastard commander wasn't here to help. Frank could hear shouts in the background, men and women calling out to each other, and the sound of orders being barked.

The man turned towards the noise, and said: "Wait here. If you move, I will shoot you myself," before walking back to the truck. Frank was left trying to keep his hands from shaking. The police had often threatened to shoot him, but there was no humor in this man's threat. Frank gripped the steering wheel and stared at the image of their truck in the mirror. He knew they wouldn't let him go, and wondered if this Captain McIntyre had authorized them to shoot him regardless if he moved or not. The horrors they'd been fighting could have sent them over the edge, causing them to see infection and monsters where they didn't exist. The man rejoined his group, and they all rushed to the back of their vehicle, obscuring them from further observation.

Frank looked back at the personnel carrier. The screams were closer now, and now he could see plumes of smoke twisting in the air. The smell filled the air, and soon it was mixed with another smell, of singed pork. Nobody could be seen beyond the vehicle, but Frank could still hear their shouts, along with the enraged howls of the zombies.

After a cursory check of his immediate surroundings, Frank took a deep breath and opened the ambulance door, while seizing his trusty tire-iron. Without some kind of intervention, he was a dead man, so he figured he might as well see what was burning. His other motivation was to treat the soldiers' injuries, which he hoped would ingratiate him to them. He left the door open and stepped down onto the concrete overpass. The sun was setting, bathing the sky in brilliant red along the smog-filled horizon. The smoke had begun to burn his throat and eyes, but he walked towards it anyway; he needed to see what was going on. The smell of cooking meat persisted. He'd forgotten how long it had been since his last meal, and his stomach grumbled its displeasure to him, in spite of his better judgment. The nightmarish screams and shouts twisted into a hellish cacophony, like a dread symphony composed in Hell itself.

Frank drew himself towards the edge of the overpass, and looked down. There was a swarm of zombies below—the biggest he'd seen yet—and they were massing at the base of the on-ramp. While he and Del had dodged groups of four or five in Sunnyside, nothing could have prepared him for the sight of dozens, maybe over a hundred, in the same place. They had homogenized into one mass of people, individual characteristics whitewashed away by the masks of blood and gore smeared over their bodies.

A wave of heat rolled past him, drying the sweat of nerves and exertion from his skin. Then a renewed series of screams slammed into him, the sound wave reverberating through his chest. He moved to the side of the military vehicle and peeked around the edge. Bile rushed into his throat; his indomitable fortitude had finally met its match. The ramp was covered in burned, dead husks, but many of the things still moved, crawling towards the humans as they burned. The flesh melted off a burned hand that grasped at the nozzle of a flamethrower that was wielded by a tall, strong woman, her face obscured by a mask. The rest of the team stood back from her, guns at the ready. Beyond, Frank could see wave upon wave of ruined humanity, surging towards them. He swallowed, hard, and checked to make sure the way back to the ambulance was secure. There didn't appear to be any zombies that way. Frank wasn't sure why he called them zombies, but the name seemed to fit.

The fiends closed in, while howling and screaming for human flesh and blood. Frank clutched the tire-iron to his chest. He couldn't look away.

Volleys of liquid flame erupted from the

flamethrower, and its raw heat licked hungrily at Frank's face. The fire moved as though it was alive, engulfing zombies as they came. Each wave of new monsters grew closer before being immolated by the inferno. Their cries were deafening, as though they could still feel pain. One small zombie leapt out at the woman with the flamethrower from behind a much larger, burning companion. The woman took a step backwards before the little monster slammed itself into her, causing her to steer the still-active flamethrower into her companions. Now they screamed too as they were engulfed in flames, running back and forth until finally collapsing. The others with guns began firing into the mass of zombies.

Frank backed up, realizing that he would be the next victim in their sights. The creatures, some of whom had burning limbs or clothes, advanced on the remaining men. Frank could see the bastard who had interrogated him go down under a mass of the undead. Guilt-tinged relief passed through him. He was free to go.

Frank ran back to the ambulance, his lungs and legs rebelling against the exertion. He climbed inside and started the engine. The mirrors showed that the creatures had broken through the army defense, and he knew they could move faster than he could. A skinny male zombie broke away from the pack and leapt against Frank's vehicle, gripping the steel doorframe. Frank accelerated and the ambulance lurched into motion. He picked up the tire-iron and slammed it against the monster's hands. It shrieked and swung at him. Frank dodged and slammed the breaks. The fiend flew forward, shattering the front mirror and landing beside the ambulance. Frank began to back up, intending to crush this zombie, just like he had his friend Marvin. The creature crawled to its feet, and charged again. Frank switched into drive, desperate to escape. The thing jumped at him, but it missed the window as Frank accelerated, grasping into the empty air of the cabin before falling away. The monster's hands grasped against Frank's arm. The slick sheen of sweat over his skin saved him— the creature was unable to get a grip in the few desperate seconds it had before he gained enough speed to pull away.

"Fuck!" Frank yelled, looking down at his arm. The skin hadn't been broken; he was intact and the fiend hadn't managed to claw him. He hammered his fist against the steering wheel, and let loose a celebratory cheer.

He was going to escape! He would be damned if he was going to let any goons take him down. There was a deep pang of guilt at his elation, however. He was the only survivor—Haley, Marvin, Del, Gerald were all lost to the mysterious, and spreading disease.

He continued to drive towards the country. He was going to make sure nobody would find him. If it was airborne, as he suspected after the attack at the police station, then he needed to get as far away from civilization as possible. He considered warning people in the towns he came across on his way west, but he doubted that any good deed on his part would go unpunished, especially after the events of the past two days.

He flipped on the sirens and sped towards the uninhabited nature preserve that was a few hours west of the city. It would take about a day to travel west through it, and he wanted to avoid civilization until he was sure he was clear of the capital. His ex-wife had a cabin in the western foothills, and he'd rather impose on her than wind up dead, or an abomination. It would take several days to get there, if not a week or more by the back roads. He sped towards the preserve, hoping to beat the setting sun so he could set up camp for the night. Illegal, but necessary—he needed time to think and reflect on the day's events in a safe, quiet place.

He thought about his Kelsey as he drove. If he made it back out west, he planned to visit her grave and bring her flowers. *Daisies*, he thought. *I'll get some daisies for my Kelsey, and some for my little Haley, too.*

Zombie Bedtime Stories, part 4:

Bedlam

Chapter 1

"I want my Mommy." The girl clinging to Corporal Samantha Henderson's hand choked back sobs, and looked up at her. She couldn't be more than seven, and her pale blue eyes were bloodshot and brimming with tears. Samantha had been part of a squad assigned to evacuate this large inner city elementary school. She didn't know if they were going to escape before the rioters closed in, but Samantha was determined to do her duty and get as many kids out as possible. The school was a decaying, squalid building—a leftover relic of the baby boom nearly a century before. Now, it was underfunded and in a state of disrepair Samantha found shocking, even compared to a childhood spent in state-funded boarding schools. The grey hallway dragged on ahead of them, only punctuated by the grey shadows of closed classroom doors and the occasional splash of children's art projects. Samantha sucked in a deep breath as she enjoyed the pounding of her boots on the cold granite floor. The echoes gave her the illusion of power and control, when in reality her stomach gnawed around the chill of uncertainty.

"We'll find her, but we need to get somewhere safe," Samantha said in her best impersonation of a soothing voice. She clenched her jaw as her free hand corralled a loose little boy. He recoiled at the sight of her, but she could understand why a small child might find her appearance shocking. She was a tall woman, standing at well over six feet, and dressed in the same imposing grey camouflage as the rest of the paramilitary compliance squad. She wore her dark brown hair cropped short, and her full nose and thin lips were almost comical in their discordance. Her barred teeth gleamed with artificial perfection—a gift from the recruiters when she enlisted two years ago.

"Are you going to fight the bad guys?" the boy asked in a hushed voice. His wide eyes scanned her face for an instant before falling to the empty hallway behind them.

Samantha cracked the boy a wicked smile, exposing more of her straight white teeth. "You bet. They'll never know what hit them!" She wore the bravado like it was a second skin. With it, she made her strength into her beauty, an art that didn't come easily to most. In truth, she didn't want to go out there. Although kids were certainly not her strong point, what little she knew of the situation made her grateful to have been assigned to searching the lower levels of the building. Summer school and various camps were in session, thus class sizes were small, meaning that the school was only operating at a fraction of its capacity. This job was better than digging in, and waiting for the rioters to come. She didn't relish spending yet another afternoon begging an indifferent higher power to make the dissidents listen to reason. Secretly, she hoped that she wouldn't need to face down a mob like the one that had swallowed her parents alive over a decade ago.

"What are they doing?" the girl asked as they walked by a classroom door that hung slightly ajar. The question snapped Samantha away from the dark place, and back into the present crisis. Memories of the Second Revolt could wait. She chewed on the inside of her lip as she sucked in another cleansing breath. The hallway was very well soundproofed, but a nightmarish blend of ghoulish screams, gunfire and shouting trickled through the open door.

Samantha gazed out the window, and her heart sank. They looked to be setting up another barrier, with more equipment being dropped off from the helicopters they were using to evacuate the elementary school to their base. She'd spent the better part of the morning helping to keep the kids calm, and making sure none of them ran off into the blades of a helicopter. She wasn't sure how Captain McIntyre intended to get all those people off the roof or the kids back to their parents, but she knew he would find a way. He inspired her—no natural disaster was too much for him, and no riot was enough to make him question his allegiance to the State. She considered him to be the essential avatar of a patriot. She other hand, found herself cynical of the policies she saw enacted around her, but she saw Captain Remus McIntyre as the embodiment of the perfect soldier—an ideal she strove to emulate. He expressed no doubts, and exuded an aura of tangible confidence in his decisions and the policies they protected. "They're keeping us safe, so we can hide until Captain McIntyre makes the bad people leave us alone," she told the girl, her own faith bolstered by the knowledge that he would know what to do. That certainty always warmed her, and never failed to guide Samantha's resolve in difficult situations. The nagging voice in the back of her head taunted her—he didn't save her parents—but she ignored it and imagined kicking the thought over the edge of a ravine. The captain had saved countless thousands more that day, Samantha included.

The answer calmed the young girl's breathing, and Samantha made a mental note to close and secure the remaining classroom doors before she made her next run. She'd been with the Peacemakers for two years—long enough to know that innocent children shouldn't have to see what happened when a dangerous and frightening riot required expert intervention. Her own haunted memories could attest to that.

They rounded the corner to the staircase, and Samantha held the door open for her two young charges. "Okay, let's run as fast as we can to the top!" She'd found that making the required tactical maneuvers into a game was the easiest way to coax kids into running up the fire escape, and overcome their natural resistance to breaking the "no going on the roof" rule. The two children bounded up the stairs, and she followed behind, careful not to trample into them. She could take the stairs two or three at a time if she wanted to, but she didn't want to lose sight of them. The blandness of the stairwell seemed to keep the kids calm, and the challenge of running to the top burned off their nervous energy. She wished she could be as easily distracted from the reality of the situation. She'd helped put down enough riots to know that this was a bad one— officers and service people had already been killed. It was going to get uglier, and while she didn't understand why this school needed to be evacuated, she had her orders. This was preferable to pelting unarmed civilians with rubber bullets, water cannons and neural stunners, at least. She shuddered at the thought of angry red welts carved into exposed flesh, and the wails of the freshly paralyzed masses writhing on the ground. In a small way, the kids reminded her of herself and her brother. They, too, had escaped from an angry mob in a day of adrenaline and triumph turned into swirling despair. Hopefully, they would both have parents to go home to.

The warmth that came with climbing four flights of stairs spread through her legs, and her breathing settled the ravenous butterflies gnawing at her stomach's core. Her macabre thoughts floated away into the summer's breeze. Samantha loved to run—the world made more sense when she was exercising. The endorphins would flow; they granted her the focus and clarity to adapt to the ever-changing demands of her job, and to her hidden inner darkness. The two children were trying to race each other up the stairwell. She saw no harm in letting them continue, in fact, she envied their single-minded ability to live in the moment. Samantha never wanted children of her own, but she didn't mind measured doses of their company, at least now that she towered over them.

Gasping and wheezing, her two charges made it to the top of the stairs and turned to cast their triumphant smiles down on her. "I won!" the boy announced, while the girl tugged at the door that opened onto the roof.

"You ran very fast, that's so good!" Samantha told him, grinning and clasping her hands in front of her. The door creaked open and a crack of light shone through.

"Don't you get tired?" the girl asked, struggling to catch her breath. Her tears were gone now, and she looked up at Samantha with wide eyes, pushing all her weight against the door in a valiant effort to hold it open.

"No, I am a secret robot. We don't get tired," Samantha said, setting her hands on her narrow hips. The boy stared at her, transfixed, his mouth agape.

The door pulled the rest of the way open, revealing the lean figure of Captain Remus McIntyre. He looked down at the two children, and said: "I see you're giving out our top secrets again, Henderson." The captain was a man of forty, which made him around two decades older than Samantha. He had a smooth, easy way of talking that lulled people into a sense of security. The world's problems never touched the man—even when he was tasked with fixing them—and his face had only just begun to be graced by lines of worry and age. His brown eyes and hair shone in the mid-day sun, and a sheen of sweat glistened over his tanned skin. There was a new hollowness in his eyes, but Samantha drank in his presence all the same.

"Yes, I'm afraid I needed to tell them, Captain. They already figured out my cover," she said, blinking as her eyes adjusted to the light. She wished she hadn't forgotten her sunglasses at the base, but there had been little warning before they were whisked away on the two-hour convoy to the capital. Their rural retreat put them within mere hours of many metropolitan sectors, which is why it was selected for their base. It also made it harder for the dissidents to interfere with their training and deployment.

"No harm done, this time," he said with a playful half-smile, and stooped down to the kids' height. The boy sank behind the girl, and the captain continued: "Are you both okay?" he asked, projecting a deep empathy in his voice. Samantha envied his ease with children, and watched, hoping to pick up some pointers as she awaited her new instructions.

"Uh-huh," the girl said, and the boy peeked out from behind her long enough to give a shy nod.

Remus reached out and took her hand. "What's your name?" he asked.

"I'm Tiffany," she said, looking at the ground.

"I'm Kevin," the boy blurted out, and he shuffled out from behind Tiffany's diminutive figure.

"Well Tiffany and Kevin, now that you've been saved by our amazing secret robot, you get to go on a helicopter ride while we make the city safe again. How does that sound?"

Kevin's face lit up, while Tiffany seemed despondent. "Is my mom coming?" she asked.

"They're on their way, but don't worry, your vice principle Mrs. Tyler will be with you until they get here," he said. "You don't want to miss the fun, do you?" he asked.

The girl shook her head, and the boy returned to staring at the ground. "Captain, how many more are missing?" Samantha asked.

"There are five left unaccounted for, according to the attendance records Mrs. Tyler gave me. Three boys and two girls. Go look for them. The staff are checking the upper floors, so give the ground floor another pass. I'll take care of these two while we wait for the next evac to get here."

"Understood, Captain," she saluted, spinning on her heel and venturing back down into the dark staircase.

There were only five left. Then, she would have to face down the angry population once again.

Chapter 2

Samantha stood in the middle of the deserted principal's office—one of the few places she hadn't checked. Its barred windows overlooked an asphalt playground, punctuated with rusting bits of whatever play equipment was deemed safe and litigation-proof. The swings sat dismantled, the iron frames rusting in the summer heat. Its comfortable air conditioning and new carpets were in direct contrast to the sweltering heat and tiled floors that she had encountered in the rest of the building, especially now that the mid-day heat had set in. She could imagine the administrators sitting at their wooden desks, making decisions for the staff and students without ever having to leave their climate-controlled bubble. She hated that. True leaders, like the captain, weren't opposed to bearing the same discomforts as their charges. If anything, Remus would sacrifice his own comfort for the good of the unit.

She moved from room to room, deliberate and methodical in her search for the five missing stragglers. The office was a logical place to go for a child who found herself separated from the rest of her group. She called out to anyone who might be listening, hoping that her voice would reach the ears of one of the missing kids and entice them out of hiding. She wanted to be able to look Captain McIntyre straight in the eyes, and say that she did her best, and that where were no lost kids on the first floor. She wondered why the administrators had refused to search the ground floor themselves. Perhaps it was cowardice. If the rioters wanted to loot the school, anyone on the ground floor would be a target. Often the Peacemakers were called to protect schools; the more militant rioters saw schools as easy targets for hostage taking. Just like her school had been.

She shook her head to clear the memories, and moved toward the exit to the main hallway. Nobody had replied to her calls, so she decided that she should give the washrooms one final pass. She wished the administrators had agreed to give her a master key—that way she could lock any doors that she had verified clear and save her a great deal of time in the process. She grit her teeth and continued the search. She winced in remembered pain as she walked past the lockers. Samantha found herself running her tongue across her new teeth, to make sure they were still there.

She paused just inside the main entrance, and looked out at the barricade the Peacekeepers had erected. She could recognize her friends and bunkmates by the way they walked and moved—a benefit of years of intense training. Distant gunfire peppered the air, and she watched her comrades argue over the placement of concrete blockades. A large part of her wished she was out there with her friends, doing what she did best—protecting. She sighed, wiping the sweat from her brow as she tried to fathom how teachers and children could learn and concentrate in this heat.

The bathrooms were neat and clean, a fact that had more to do with the school being evacuated early in the day than the fastidiousness of the custodial staff. She wracked her mind for some notion where of where a kid might hide. She just didn't know. As she exited the last of the washrooms and re-entered the hallway, she could hear a sound that sounded like screaming coming from outside, but the outcry was more feral and desperate. *It's probably a street fight*, she told herself. *Real riots have megaphones and chanting.*

She went on about her duty, ignoring the screams. The sounds persisted, even penetrating the closed classroom doors. Samantha shivered, in spite of the sweltering heat. As Samantha stalked the halls, she was still careful to pick a path far from the dented assortment of lockers—an old habit, borne out of necessity. The empty halls reminded her of the many times she'd run through her school, deliberately late, to avoid the sneers and other, more brutal attacks from the other students. The crook in her flat nose was one memory made real, frozen on her face every time she looked in the mirror. It still mocked her to this day. Her teeth had been easy to replace, but Samantha hadn't decided if she'd sign on for another ten years just for a nose-job. School administrators had done nothing to curb the violence against her. They'd implied that she somehow deserved it, or that she'd done something to draw the ire of her fellow students. Neither was true—Samantha couldn't change her appearance, no matter how much she tried to slouch in her chair, or how long she grew her hair. That particular attempt at assimilation had earned her a cruel nickname: *Caveman*.

Samantha had only wanted to be left alone with her books, or left in peace to jog around the school's crumbling race track. She'd joined the Peacemakers as soon as she had been able to, knowing in their company she would never be weak and alone again. They had taken that scared, hurt girl, and transformed her into a soldier. She now had purpose, a family of peers and inner strength. Nobody she worked with cared what she looked like, and they all wore the same clothes. In spite of her dour surroundings, she smiled. Neither the prune-faced teachers nor the administrators, who were caught up in their idealized perceptions of childhood, nor the students who cruelly tormented her could find her now, or hurt her ever again.

The unmistakable sound of gunfire exploded outside, startling her back into the present. This time, it was close, and she didn't want to find herself wandering a deserted school in the middle of a warzone—at least, not without her buddies. She sprinted to the door of the first street-facing classroom, and flung it open.

She waded through the too-narrow rows of desks and chairs, trying to peer past the dying cedar hedge that blocked much of the view, but the sounds were distinct, and terrifying. She could hear ghoulish and incoherent howls and screams—more animal than human. Samantha had never encountered anything like it. A nervous pit formed in her stomach. Another volley of gunfire erupted from behind the shrub, causing her to jump. Deadly force was seldom needed in modern dealings with civil unrest. Her comrades, people she'd known for years, were shouting and barking orders at each other, their voices sounding urgent and afraid, even through the sealed glass windows.

Samantha knew she had to do something.

She broke into a run, knocking over several desks in her frantic rush to get out of the classroom. Captain McIntyre was on the roof; he would know what was going on. She slammed the door shut behind her and ran full-tilt toward the staircase. She doubted any children would stay hidden after overhearing the intensity of the battle being waged outside. Crashing into the door to the narrow staircase, she fumbled it open and sprinted up the flights of stairs three steps at a time, driven by the need to protect her friends.

Sweat dripped down her brow as she mounted the final series of stairs, and then she threw her weight against the roof's stubborn door. Crashing through, the flash of intense daylight blinded her, but the unmistakable beating of helicopter blades pounded through the air, punctuated by the sound of gunfire coming from below. Trying to orient herself, Samantha remained still until her eyes adjusted to the stronger light. It wouldn't be good to wander into the business end of a helicopter, or a wandering kid. Fragments of conversation drifted in the hot air, but it was difficult to distinguish between the singing of frightened children from the frantic shouts of men and women, and the shrieks and screams emanating from the street below.

Her eyes adjusted to the glare of the hot June sun, but they stung from a new irritant that she hadn't noticed before—smoke. It was the kind of fine haze that might herald an oncoming riot. Ignoring the smoke, she scanned the people on the rooftop. Captain McIntyre was in a corner, talking into a radio handset, his foot propped against on the roof's shallow edge as he gazed into the confusion unfolding below. Mrs. Tyler and the others stood safely away from the copter and the ledge and a large group of children sat at their feet, holding each other's hands and singing songs.

Samantha approached them. "Have all of the missing children been located?" she asked.

"Yes, and they have been for quite a while now," Mrs. Tyler said, her voice cracking through wrinkled lips.

Mrs. Tyler was an older woman, whose lips were always drawn and puckered together. Her hair was dyed burgundy—the color of denial and desperation in aging women. Samantha suspected that Mrs. Tyler was a woman who had never truly been young, judging from the angry string of frown lines that savagely cut though her face.

"That's good, but why wasn't I informed of that?"

"You would have figured it out by yourself, *eventually*."

"Excuse me, ma'am?" Samantha couldn't believe the woman's hostility.

"I'm not about to send somebody educated down there. That's what *your* kind is for." The woman's lined mouth frowned and twisted the papery skin into a glaring mask.

"I don't think I deserve that. We serve the people, and keep them safe."

"I'm sure that's what your captain told you to think. Now, run along and get more orders to follow, before you contaminate more of our children with notions of glory and power," the old woman said with a sneer. It was impossible to comprehend how she could feel such animosity toward people in uniform. They were protecting her from a certain, horrible, fate!

"How am I contaminating children?" Samantha had to restrain herself from the fleeting urge to fling the miserable woman off the roof. She sounded so much like the teachers in her own high school, who had tried to discourage her from enlisting. They'd even mocked her in front of the class, for being too stupid and poor to attend college. She hadn't been able to speak up then, but she could now.

"College is where young people belong, not fighting wars and hurting innocent civilians. Now you've gone and put ideas about being a super soldier robot into Tiffany and Kevin's heads. It's going to take us weeks of counseling to get them back on track to integrating properly with society and away from your recruiters."

Samantha was very grateful to not be attending this school. "That is your opinion, ma'am. We save lives, and shape young men and women. *Good* young men and women."

"Amen, Henderson," said a deep, familiar voice behind her. Mrs. Tyler shot her a final poisonous glare and turned back to one of her perpetually-nodding cronies.

"Captain!" Samantha turned and saluted.

"You know better than to be formal with me, Sammy. Come over here for a second. I'm sure these fine, *educated* ladies can handle a few kids on their own." His voice retained the same easy, flowing manner that it always had, but there was a new hardness in his eyes that she'd never seen before, even when times were at their worst. It was doubtful that he appreciated Mrs. Tyler's anti-military candor, but he wasn't the type of person to take the prejudices of others personally. They'd heard it all before, at other schools.

"With pleasure, Sir," she said flashing him a toothy grin. Whatever the problem was, they would solve it. They walked to the edge of the roof where Remus had been standing before. The scent of smoke and fire was stronger, and more unworldly howls and screams floated through the air. Straining, she could hear familiar voices—those of her friends and coworkers, distressed and shouting. Thankfully, there seemed to be a lull in the gunfire. Her smile faded then, and she stood at attention, waiting for him to speak. Samantha's hands remained glued to her sides while she chewed the inside of her lip. She gazed down into the school yard while the bright sun roasted against her skin.

The captain's eyes searched the distant horizon for a moment, before her finally spoke. "Things are bad, Sammy. Worse than we thought—we might not be able to stop this one." His voice was hushed, and withdrawn. It was one of the few times she'd seen him without his characteristic smile.

"We'll stop it. We always do, Sir," she said, trying to tap into the infectious enthusiasm the man always radiated. Her words rang hollow without the amplifying force of his resolve. They festered inside her own mind as memories of her parents' mangled bodies surfaced. She shoved them back down.

"Not this time. This one is different. We have to use lethal force. I don't like it, and worse, Cartwright doesn't like it." He spoke slowly, weighing his words. Major Cartwright was the notorious public face of the military's new science directorate—Compliance Studies. Usually, he was off devising new ways to stun civilians or pressing results out of the few scientists the country had left. For reasons that had never been revealed to Samantha, Remus hated the man. She did know that Cartwright was always forcing prototypes on them, rather than just letting them do their jobs.

"Well, at least you agree about something. If we can work together, we can solve this and go home, right?"

"It seems not. He's got people out there rounding up protestors—dead or alive. The Peacemakers' job is to quarantine the city and keep the rioters contained in here." His quiet voice was overtaken by the hurried shouts below.

"What are your orders?" Despite Mrs. Tyler's earlier goading, she knew her place in the chain of command, and she intended to do her duty.

"The school is empty; we have no reason to stay here. Once the last helicopters are gone, I want you to go with Richards and Pike. You're going to use Cemfoam to seal the city's western highways off, and then I want you to drive back to the base and take careful note of the people and countryside, anything that seems out of the ordinary."

"Yes, Sir." She was proud that he'd chosen her— she was seldom picked for more than simple pacification duties or being put in situations where the only requirement was looking scary. It was exciting to be the person chosen to deploy the anti-vehicle barriers. She could imagine using a giant hose to spray the liquid onto the ground, and the foam would grow and harden into a cement-like structure within only minutes. The resultant barriers were soluble, if you had access to the proper chemical. The remembered scent of Cemfoam stung her nostrils. She'd trained for this for over two years, and it was finally time for her to prove herself.

"Now, listen to me Sammy. These aren't normal people out there. They're crazy and vicious. Don't let them near you, and keep your mind on the mission." He tapped his forehead as he spoke. The paternalistic, calm voice was back.

The knot of worry that had tightened in Samantha's stomach was calmed by the glow of his words. "I won't let you down, Captain."

"Good. Now, wait here with me while Richards and Pike set up the vehicle. They've done this in live situations before. Follow their lead and you'll do fine."

The rhythmic beat of helicopter blades suddenly morphed into a high pitched whine. Turning, Samantha watched as the copter took off, and threw out an exaggerated wave. *I hope Kevin and Tiffany will remember we're all still human, uniform or no*, she thought. *Besides, I'm the top secret robot. I can do anything!*

Chapter 3

Samantha sat in the passenger seat of their large grey hybrid personnel carrier; the vehicle had been modified from the original design to include a generous tank of Cemfoam and all the tools needed for rapid barrier creation. The modifications left little room for passengers and she found herself crammed up against the window next to Sergeant Pike, a smiling but soft and lumpish man in his thirties. He could hold his own against anyone, despite his generous girth and diminutive height. Richards was driving, his face contorted into its usual angry frown. He was not as tall as Samantha, but still above average and his lean figure was wrapped in layers of muscle. He could be a pleasant enough fellow, if you caught him alone and off-duty. At work, he was the personification of duty-bound professionalism.

None of them spoke; they had witnessed the unthinkable in their harrowing departure from the besieged elementary school. Because of the approaching mob, they'd borne helpless witness to a gruesome and bloody battle and watched friends die. They needed time to think, but they also had a job to do, and many more lives depended on keeping a clear head, and those *crazies* bottled up within the city boundaries.

The words "get that flamethrower up here" repeated over and over again in Samantha's mind. The rioters—vicious, cruel monstrosities in human form—had begun to pour over the school's low barrier. The terrible scene tortured her. Dylan was quartered by unarmed civilians in an instant. It was unspeakable—how was it even possible? She was much stronger than the average person, and even she could only manage to dislocate a limb, not tear a leg from the hip socket of a struggling full-grown man. The evidence to the contrary had flashed before her eyes. She'd fought junkies before, not even super-Z made people that violent, or powerful. All she could do was hope that all the mayhem that was going on hadn't been brought on by the next great designer drug—for once, she wished she had one of Major Cartwright's damned prototypes. He could be working on an antidote already. They needed an edge, or the outcome could only be many dead on both sides; it was a possibility she did not relish.

The rest of the encounter had been even more terrifying. In response to Dylan's dismemberment, Lasalle, an intimidating giant of a man, had stepped out with a flamethrower. They hadn't even flinched at his mandated warning blasts; they were too busy devouring Dylan and the other fallen, whole. *They had eaten human flesh!* But the horror of this cannibalistic feast was only seconded by the waves of people charging straight into Lasalle's inferno, paying no heed to their own safety.

Eventually, the charging throng extinguished itself on their intense fire. Dense smoke hung in the air, along with the nauseating smell of burned flesh. They drove out, crushing corpses beneath their tires and feeling the sickening crunch of brittle body parts snapping against the bottom of their vehicle. Samantha's palms were dented by her short-cut fingernails, and she'd chewed her thumbnail down to the quick.

After their escape, the streets were vacant of human life as they drove onwards toward city limits. Squirrels bolted into trees as they approached, only stopping when they'd climbed to the highest limb. A too-quiet wrongness permeated the city; it was as though all the residents had suddenly packed up and moved away. Curtains were drawn over closed windows, in defiance of the day's heat. No children played in the yards, and no pets languished in the shade of trees. Cars sat empty by the side of the road, and they hadn't passed a single city bus along their route. It was so idyllic, yet the events of the past hour tarnished the glorious sunshine and peaceful surroundings.

"We're so fucked." Pike spat out the words, staring straight ahead.

"Why's that?" Samantha asked. She didn't know why he was worried—they were in the suburbs, far from the inner city school and the horror they'd seen, which would become the source of their many inevitable nightmares. Samantha had always been plagued by bad dreams—ever since that day when the Revolt started. The public called them protestors, but she knew it was a revolution.

"Ignore him Sammy, just do your job and we'll be back behind concrete walls on base in no time." Richards said.

"Am I the only person here who saw dozens of people run head first into a damned flamethrower?" Pike's jowls shook as he spoke.

"No, but we have a job to do. We can process *that* on our own time. We need to get the Cemfoam down so nobody else has to die like that." Richards' voice was strained, and his grip on the wheel tightened.

"Remus could have at least sent us out here with a flamethrower." Pike grumbled as he stretched, kicking Samantha in the shin. Her eyes narrowed for an instant, before she drew a deep breath and unclenched her fist.

"So now you're mad we don't have a flamethrower, Pike?" she asked, knowing that it would be easy to provoke him into a rant of some kind. At least that would break the continuous loop of memories.

"We're the smallest truck; you bet every other group has a flamethrower. How are we going to keep dozens of the bastards away from us if all we have are our side arms?"

"Work faster, then. Worry less." Richards' reply was distant and resigned.

"It's not like we actually have to stop anyone. Come on Pike, it takes five to seven minutes to set up a barrier. We'll be long gone before they figure out we're even up there." She held her voice steady and spoke slow, just like she'd seen Captain McIntyre give his orders and instructions.

"That's training, Sammy. You never know what will happen out there; the hose and pump could fuck up and we'd be stuck moving the Cemfoam in little plastic cups from the garbage."

"It happens more often than you think, Sammy." Pike could never resist an opportunity to be demotivating.

"Jeez you guys, you'd think the captain ordered us to redirect a river or something. It's just three highway exits. It's not like there's another way out of the suburbs. If the pump breaks, then we'll just use Pike's mouth to spray it." Samantha couldn't help laughing at the mental image of Pike's jowls shaking as he spit the foamy concoction onto the road. Of course, Cemfoam was toxic and corrosive, and came with strict instructions to avoid skin contact and ingestion.

"Yeah, good thing Remus sent you with us to do the damn thinking, Sammy." Richards' voice lightened, but Pike appeared to sulk, his face drooping even lower than usual.

Samantha returned to staring out the passenger-side window, watching the warm breeze tease bushes and trees. It was such a beautiful day, not fitting for so much bloodshed. On her day, it had been raining.

Chapter 4

Samantha peered over the edge of the overpass, scanning past the tufts of dead grass for a sign of life. Nothing moved; it was as though she, Pike and Richards were the last people left on the planet. The occasional helicopter dotted the horizon. Watching them fly off into the perfect blue sky caused a pang of sadness to stab through her awareness. Would life return to normal, or would this renewed revolt herald the end of civilization? Samantha didn't know the answer, only that she would do everything she could to put things right. "All clear down this side," she said, drawing a deep breath. She wasn't green by any means, but today's events had shaken her more than she wanted to admit.

"Good. Let's get started before I melt," Pike said, sweat already running down the grooves in his face and soaking through his uniform. Richards stood a short distance ahead, standing watch where the overpass began to slope downwards into the city streets.

"At least there are only three exits," Samantha said as she swung open the back doors of the carrier, exposing a long pressure tank filled with Cemfoam, the pumping system in the back and a long coil of hose.

"For once I'm grateful for those snobby suburban parasites. Fuckers don't want traffic? Now they get to stay locked in with the freaks. Take the hose Sammy, I'll work the pump."

Samantha took up the end of the hose. It was less worn than the ones she'd trained with, and she held it fast under her right arm. It was about twice the thickness of a fire hose, and the heavy rubber composite bit at the bare skin and fine hair on her arms. She moved to a flat steel segment of the overpass—she wanted to get a good, straight barrier set up that would require as little adjustment and refinement as possible.

There was a slight kickback as the compound began to flow out of the nozzle. The foam was a creamy white color and had a frothy consistency, like whipped cream. The smell told a different story, and the familiar acrid sting burned Samantha's nostrils as she held the hose steady. She directed the flow over the metal seam in the road, keeping her pace slow and deliberate. There needed to be at least half a foot of foam on the ground for it to grow and harden at a level that would stop a car or truck.

She glanced forward; Richards was pacing, but she saw no indication that anyone was coming. There were only four lanes on this overpass—it was more of a service road than anything. Arriving at the end, she turned the crank on the nozzle and the flow tapered off, the final drips narrowly missing her right boot.

Richards jogged back toward the truck, jumping over the expanding Cemfoam. The speed and efficiency of the process continued to amaze Samantha with every increment that the wall grew. It would harden in mere minutes, and keep vehicles from escaping the city. Richards started the truck as she and Pike scrambled to get the hose stowed away. One wrong move could trigger the hardening reaction, bursting the pipe and ending the mission.

After securing the back doors, they ran to the front, eager to get to the second stop and closer to a completed assignment. The GPS unit would guide them, taking a route outside the city. None of them were local to the capital, and she hoped that they wouldn't get lost. Climbing in after Pike, she buckled up and they sped toward their next stop.

It couldn't all be this easy.

***

Skyscrapers dominated the skyline at their next stop—colloquially called Heaven's Highway. The downtown core that housed the area's prominent business headquarters was reputed to be immaculate and a testament to urban design and management. Samantha decided that assessment must have been the local propaganda department working overtime. She'd seen her fair share of urban scenery and riots, and she'd found that this metropolis wasn't unique. Still, it was far from the worst city she'd visited—that place qualified as a ghost town filled with malcontents, rather than a proper city.

Once again, Richards took watch—his single sidearm provided a small sense of reassurance. Samantha was a proverbial sitting duck while she sprayed the Cemfoam. Pike would have her back, too, but this was a major highway—ten lanes for her to cover. It was an arduous task under the punishing mid-afternoon sun. That drug that had affected the population—or whatever *it* was—needed to be contained before it spread to other cities. Samantha hoped that a *special* place would be found in prison for whoever started this, one where the punishment would reflect the magnitude of the crime. It was the only hell that mattered.

After a cursory glance from side-to-side, Samantha readied herself in the far left lane. There was very little that looked different from the last exit—a highway was just a highway, after all—but the grass here was a patchy green, rather than all-dead like at the edge of the suburbs. She also didn't have a metal bar embedded into the pavement to guide her this time, so she needed to factor that into her estimates. The bright sun glinted off the nozzle of the hose, and she felt the familiar kick of the pump as it turned on.

Twisting toward the extreme left, she flicked on the nozzle and stooped down for better control over the viscous, flowing liquid. It occurred to her that it would have been interesting to set up a camera, simply to capture the entire barrier at different stages of deployment. She'd left her camera at the base, though … and besides, there wasn't time. Riot duty was seldom photogenic, and besides, she never liked how she looked in riot gear. Some soldiers—like Pike—collected pictures of themselves from the news. Those photos captured the more unpleasant aspects of their line of work. Samantha found it too macabre to contemplate; it was too much like celebrating the pain of others. She wanted to live in a world without riots, one where everyone was safe and could be free to enjoy complete order and security.

Beads of sweat dripped down her face, and the heated tingle on the back of her neck and arms betrayed the burning of her fair skin. She muttered a quiet curse— she tended to blister and hated being at the mercy of anyone sadistic enough to slap her sunburn. The hard rubber of the hose stuck and pulled at her exposed arms, but she fought the discomfort and persevered. Her breathing fell into a constant series of deep breaths—much like with running, she needed to push through this pain. Turning back toward her work, she noted that four lanes had already been filled with the Cemfoam. *That's forty-percent*, she thought. It was easier to appreciate goals and get through a task when she imagined her progress as percentages.

A series of harsh, animalistic screams rose through the air, the decibels competing with those of the Cemfoam pump. Samantha jumped. She momentarily lost control of the nozzle, splattering a jagged pile of Cemfoam in front of her. She looked up, and regained her composure. She continued to pour, moving as quickly as the flow would allow. Straight, neat lines be damned. *They* were nearby.

"Shit!" Richards' voice carried well, and he was running back toward the vehicle. Samantha did a lane-check. *Sixty percent.*

"Fuck!" Pike shouted, and rushed up to her. "Keep going, we'll take care of it," he said before sprinting to meet Richards, sidearm in hand. She couldn't see anything out of the ordinary, as the drop-off was blocking her view.

The howls drew closer and the first shots echoed through the empty air, drowning out the crazed noises. The reprieve lasted for only an instant. She swallowed, hard. Richard and Pike made a mad dash toward the dried and solidified end of her barrier. She continued her pace, and tightened her grip on the hose despite the pain of it rubbing against her skin. Eighty percent, which translated into only two or three more minutes of work. But, those minutes could be an eternity if the bastards got to her.

Pike and Richards dove behind the barrier. "They're coming, about a dozen! Keep going and run like fuck once you get that last section down. We'll cover you!" Pike held his voice steady, and his eyes wide open.

A small crowd of people crested the ascent of the highway, charging down the middle of the road. They were an eclectic group—some young, some old, even a pre-teen girl. With the exception of the girl, they were all dressed for office work. Bright smears of blood marred their perfect white work shirts, and popped buttons exposed soiled undergarments or pale, bloated bodies. Their faces were coated in dry and drying blood. It was like a cheesy horror movie, but in broad daylight, in the here and now of the real world. Samantha never liked what happened to military types in those movies.

A hail of gunfire tore through the air, pounding through the frontrunners. They dropped to the ground, but continued to crawl forward toward them. Samantha's heart raced, blood coursing through her ringing ears. The boundaries of her consciousness frayed and her head spun. More gunshots fired. The survivors leapt over the bodies of the fallen. The remaining monsters were closing in, and fast. Five of the remaining group headed toward Richards and Pike. Three charged straight for Samantha, including the little girl. Her ponytail swung as she ran, and her high voice screamed and snarled the most heinous of their vocalizations.

Samantha remained at her post. There wasn't much of the wall left to complete, but the monstrosities were going to beat her to it. The two adults that had zeroed in on her dropped in a bloody percussion of bullets—a portly man's bald head exploded, showering brain matter all over his companions. Samantha flinched. The *others* ignored their fresh garnishments, still transfixed by their ultimate goal: Samantha. She could hear cries and shouts among the frantic gunfire—human sounds. A sideways glance told her that the other creatures had reached the barrier and were closing in on Pike and Richards. She was alone with the two creatures; things made in the image of humanity but robbed of the capacity for empathy and reason.

Samantha screamed and cranked the hose's flow meter to maximum capacity. A slurry of Cemfoam erupted from the nozzle. The foamy grey liquid slapped the ground so hard that it splashed onto her boots and pants. Now was not the time to worry about how to pass inspection, or concern herself about damage to the pump and hose. Right now, she needed to do whatever it would take to save her life. She wasn't going to end up like Dylan!

She braced herself by taking a deeper stance, and she heaved the stream toward the two approaching freaks.

She knew it didn't have sufficient force to hurt them, but maybe she could slow them down. Her aim was perfect—she hit her target, a petite brunette with a gaping, untended scar running down the left side of her face. The woman howled as the thick fluid coated her clothes and ran down her legs. Samantha ran backwards as fast as she could without the risk of tripping, and directed the flow toward the little girl with the ponytail. Samantha couldn't afford to be merciful; it was kill or be killed. Gunshots still fired, but they were muted by the haze of adrenaline and desperation. She bellowed her pain and rage until her voice was hoarse, but kept on screaming until tears ran down her cheeks.

The stream of Cemfoam hit the girl in the face, prompting a gurgling howl as she inhaled the sticky glop. The compound trickled down her body, slowing as it reached the ground. The hose was now hot to the touch, and it burned Samantha's arms, but she knew holding on would be her only hope of survival. The Cemfoam was the only thing that stood between herself and certain dismemberment. Flashes of Dylan's desecrated corpse ran through her mind as she alternated the blasts between her two targets. Samantha blinked back a renewed surge of tears and gritted her teeth.

There was a sharp tug, and the hose fell away. She'd run out of length, but they were still advancing on her. The foam on their bodies was expanding and hardening in the hot sun. It would only be a matter of time before it stopped them in their tracks. Samantha recoiled from the spreading pool of Cemfoam, and then she turned and sped toward the truck. The spillage would finish the job, leaving her free to recover her gun and help her friends.

Running to the far side of the truck, she opened the door and seized her pistol, its lethal weight clicking to life. It was warm from sitting in the sun, and it burned against her aching hands. She sprinted to the front, and froze in a grotesque combination of delight and horror.

The figures had ceased their advance—held fast by the growing Cemfoam that coated their bodies. The expanding grey mass contorted limbs, stretching them to impossible angles. The snapping of bone and tearing of muscle could be heard between the gunshots.

Gunshots.

With her own threat neutralized, Samantha ran to the back of the truck to help her friends. She was greeted by a scene of gory violence—the ongoing massacre of the rest of the group that had attacked them. Pike shot at the survivors, who continued to crawl toward him, all the while hissing like demented serpents. Richards sank to the ground with his gun in his lap, and gazed at angry looking gash in his forearm.

"You guys okay?" Samantha asked, as she hopped into the back of the truck and turned off the pump. The environs returned to its former stillness. She pulled at the end of the hose to haul it back in. She didn't want to look at the human sculptures she'd created. She had turned those people to stone, like she'd summoned Medusa from the pages of some arcane spellbook.

"Fucker bit me," Richards said in a subdued voice. He gestured toward a body that lay face-down on the ground. Samantha couldn't tell if the remains belonged to a male or female; the non-descript clothes were ill-fitting and head had been reduced to a bloody mass of pulp against the pavement.

"You got him, that's what matters. Bleeding stopped yet?" Pike was walking back toward them, his face sagging even further. Hints of sunburn were evident across his soft, pale skin. Bits of bone and flesh plastered his boots and pants. Samantha gagged at the thought of having to spend three hours driving in the heat with the smell of rotting human flesh a constant reminder of what they'd been through.

"I think so. Fucker had good teeth." Richards hauled himself to his feet. He was paler, from blood loss, Samantha presumed.

Pike looked past the vehicle toward the chaos that marred her almost-straight line of Cemfoam, and burst out laughing. "Damn, Sammy. I think you missed a spot, they're still moving!"

"Shit, what?" Samantha turned away from the highway of the dead and hopped out of the truck. There was still a few feet of hose left to reel in, but she could deal with that quickly. How could they possibly still be alive after being doused in Cemfoam, a substance that was both corrosive and would break bones from the sheer force of its expansion? Only a zombie could be that resilient—even the army's genetically modified super soldiers couldn't take that kind of punishment. What a word ... zombie. It reminded her of watching horror movies with her boarding school friends and trying not to act scared. Zombies had always creeped her out, but they couldn't be real.

The zombie stalagmite had altered since she'd last looked at it, only minutes ago. The Cemfoam had lifted itself toward the sky from whatever weird angle it had coalesced on. Backs were bent at an impossible angle, but Samantha could still see movement in the limbs of the adult female she had sprayed. A loud crack sounded as an arm savagely breached the cement that was restraining it. Blood oozed from the liberated skin, and the block of Cemfoam slid off her hand onto the ground, taking most of her flesh with it.

"That's impossible," she said, her eyes bulging. The ruined, fleshless hand was twitching and grasping in the air as though it had a life of its own. Another limb snapped free, exposing an arm that had been corroded to the bone—no flesh remained as the chunks of Cemfoam fell away.

"Holy fuck!" Pike said, as he took aim. He fired into the heart of the column, shattering it into scores of smaller pieces.

Samantha dodged as one of the larger pieces flew by her head. "Shit, Pike, at least warn us!" She was about to continue berating him when the slumped, broken figure squirmed, attempting to right itself. It made no sound, and continued its tortured dance.

Two more shots fired, and the bloody half-naked body was finally still. The bile rose in her throat—this was beyond comprehension.

"Let's get the fuck out of here," she said, turning back to the truck. Pike and Richards only looked at each other and nodded. She clasped her shaking hands behind her back, and took a deep breath.

She badly wanted to go back to the base, behind tall walls and razor wire fences. Captain McIntyre would know what to do. She only knew that they would need to rename the highway now—there remained little that was heavenly about it.

Chapter 5

The sun was setting as they drove down isolated country roads on their way back to their base. Pike drove this time, and Richards sat in the middle. Neither spoke much, but Richards seemed even more withdrawn than usual. He cradled his arm in silence, and his leg trembled against her as they sat. Samantha kept her eyes on their surroundings—she'd been instructed to observe the countryside, but so far there'd been nothing to see but cows and birds. It looked normal enough from her perspective—farmland looked the same anywhere you went. She found herself taking note of the colors of the cattle, or how old the houses along the way were; anything to keep her mind of the day's events. Samantha doubted she would ever sleep soundly again. Of course she would sleep—the medic had a wonderful concoction for that— but even his pharmaceutical wizardry wouldn't be enough to suppress the dreams that were sure to follow. She didn't want to visit the psych, but it was better than being haunted by the specter of that experience. No training could have prepared a person for *that*.

Their last stop had gone well, but extensive damage had been done to the Cemfoam pump and hose. The mechanism's pressure and mix balances had lost their calibration because of the strain of remaining in operation for so long, or, at least that was Pike's best guess. They would need extensive maintenance—and worse— Samantha would have to explain to the Captain and mechanics how she had damaged them. The truck cabin had begun to reek of the adrenaline of unwashed bodies, the acrid smell of Cemfoam, and the stench of drying blood.

Samantha was restless and stir-crazy; she'd spent most of the day inside a cramped truck with Pike and Richards, who weren't terribly personable even on a good day. Samantha's legs ached for a run, where she could leave the fear and adrenaline behind in the dust. A good, hot meal would be great, as well. Richards stared straight ahead. He'd been rubbing his hands together the entire trip back, and he often shivered despite the intense heat of the waning day. How could he be cold? Both she and Pike were dripping with sweat, and the sour smell of male body odor had permeated the small cabin. Samantha wrinkled her nose and leaned toward the window. Judging by the hills that crept up along the horizon, she could tell that they weren't far from home. She just needed to endure another half-hour of these sweaty, stinky confines, before she could go eat, run and shower. Most importantly, she'd be safe behind the ten-foot tall cement walls. Zombies couldn't climb, could they? The ones she'd fought earlier sure couldn't fly, at least.

There was that damn word again; zombie. A source of a seemingly endless string of B-movies and all kinds of product lines had somehow been brought to life. But, these ones they'd seen today didn't shamble, or moan. They howled, screamed and ran with a purpose that signified more than a bottomless hunger—something more akin to the deranged rage of a rabid lion.

"What do you think they were on?" she asked, talking over Richards' never-still body. The man just could not stop shivering, and that annoyed Samantha, despite the fact that she knew he was injured.

"It wasn't super-Z, that's for fucking sure. The antidote cloud or level three stunners would have worked," Pike said, rubbing the beads of sweat from his forehead with the back of one hand.

"Fucker bit me. Why?" Richards interjected; his voice was quiet and his eyes half-closed. Samantha sighed.

Pike did more than sigh. "You're delicious. Jesus, what do you want us to say? You keep asking the same damn question." It was true; Richards' anger at the mob seemed to have dissipated into a strange form of self-pity.

"Why?"

"Aliens did it, fuck, I don't know." Samantha sighed and rolled her eyes. She and Pike were going to have to drag his sorry ass to the medic instead of dealing with their own problems.

"Aliens; that's a good one Sammy. It was fucking aliens, Richards. Now shut the fuck up."

"Yeah, aliens." The answer seemed to soothe Richards. He clasped his hand over the bite on his arm and went still.

"At least we got through to him." Samantha almost found herself wondering if it really was extraterrestrials. The idea was preposterous, but so were zombies.

"Leave it to ET to save the fucking day. I don't think it was drugs. Drugs don't make you able to break Cemfoam and survive multiple gunshot wounds. My aim isn't that bad," Pike said as he squinted off into the distance and glanced at the upcoming road signs. "Twenty minutes, thank God."

"It'll be good to be back home. No zombies *or* aliens there." Samantha was relieved that she wasn't the only one who was having trouble processing the day's events.

"Aliens!" Richards spoke so loudly that Samantha jumped. She suspected that he wasn't a fan of the zombie idea.

"I fucking hate zombie movies. The writers think we're all a bunch of stupid goons." At least she and Pike agreed on something.

"Yeah, at least in movies with aliens, the humans fight back and win. Whatever, Cartwright's probably got his eggheads working to figure this all out and the captain will have a solution for us as soon as we drive in the gates." It never hurt to be optimistic, and she reached to that place of strength inside herself to help her state her point. The voice in the back of her head, however, shoved the image of her dead parents into the forefront of her mind's eye. She swallowed and shook her head.

"I never thought that guy Cartwright would get to be a hero. He's probably even got his own pet alien now." Pike barked a hoarse laugh as he spoke.

"Some people have all the luck." Samantha looked into the beginnings of a brilliant country sunset, and wished she was anywhere else but out in the open when those zombie-alien things were roaming around.

"Yeah, my little sister serves with him as a lab tech. I hope they got this mess figured out and she's okay," Pike said, elbowing Richards in the ribs before he could say something. "We got it Richards. Aliens. Go back to sleep."

"I bet it was her that figured out this whole mess."

"That'd be my little sis alright. She wanted to be a scientist, but with all the fucking government cutbacks in grants and scholarships, the best she could hope for was to join up and train to be a lab rat." Pike's voice lowered to a growl as he spat out the words.

"That's fucked up." It wasn't an uncommon story. Unless you were born rich or had family willing to spend the rest their lives helping you pay off impossible loans, there was no way to get a higher education. Her brother had tried, and failed to secure one of the few scholarships that remained, instead opting to becoming a bookkeeping clerk rather than an accountant. It was a damn pity that all the poor folk with innate smarts got to rot in dead-end jobs.

"It's a fucking shame; that girl could change the world if somebody gave her a damn chance. At least Cartwright listens to her. I can't hate him, even if he keeps forcing those fucking contraptions of his on us."

"I wouldn't let the captain hear you say that," Samantha joked. The differences of opinion between Cartwright and McIntyre had become something of a minor legend to people in their line of work.

"Well, that's a harder problem to fix than zombies and aliens combined. They can have their stupid rivalry as long as my sister is taken care of. What does it matter if Cartwright was promoted first? Fucking officers."

Samantha expected Richards to respond, but he appeared to be fast asleep. "Your sister is more important than ego, of course."

Richards didn't respond and they continued down the country road in silence. As the setting sun lit the sky with blood red fire, Samantha returned to watching cows and thinking about aliens. She'd had enough weirdness for one day.

Chapter 6

Halogen spotlights glared their angry beams of light at them as they waited for the gate to unlock. The sun had set, leaving the sky a clear dark blue. Venus could be seen clearly, as could the waning half-moon. Samantha's legs were stiff from the strain of sitting cramped for so long, and Richards had never woken up from his last nap. Even the intense glare of the halogen bulbs that crossed his face and noises of the busy base failed to rouse him. Samantha envied him; she was jacked up from the excitement of the day, and she didn't know if she would be able to sleep at all. The medic had a tranquilizer for that, if he hadn't run out.

The gate rolled open and they drove into the base. She was going to have to spend most of the evening cleaning up, and explaining the Cemfoam pump had been damaged. She was terrified of disappointing Captain McIntyre, although she had no idea what she could have done differently. The situation didn't provide room for options. One of the bastards had taken a bite out of Richards' arm, and some of them were coming for her. She hoped the Captain would understand—he always had in the past, when she'd explained things to him. Her clean record was a matter of personal pride. Pike had told her not to worry so much, but that advice had only heightened her sense of dread. Not to mention she'd ruined her best pair of boots—it was always difficult to get the quartermaster to order the custom fit she required. Between watching friends get torn to pieces, seeing crazies charging into a flamethrower, ruining her boots with Cemfoam and Richards getting bitten, it had been a terrible day. To top it off, she had a sunburn blistering across her fair skin, but that didn't compare to the rest. Not by a long shot.

She broke from her inner monologue of despair and watched the activity of the soldiers in the base. Their movements were furtive and urgent, as though word of invading zombies and aliens had already spread. Faces were pinched and drawn, and shoulders were hunched. The gut-churning effects of trepidation and fear surged back to the surface, and suppositions of horrible tidings raced through Samantha's mind. After a brief stop to return their weapons to storage, Samantha and her entourage continued toward their final parking spot.

They pulled into a garage and Pike cut the engine. The silence was surreal and it permeated the empty room. Samantha hopped out of the truck, relieved to be breathing fresh air again. She'd grown used to the stench, but its absence was welcome and she took a deep breath and stretched. Relief washed through her tired, sunburned limbs. She looked around the garage—there were no mechanics were to be seen, it was just them. At least she wouldn't have to see the mechanic's reactions when the back of the carrier was opened and the damage was revealed. Tools and toolboxes lined the walls, and bright fluorescent lights glared overhead; the place had the look of an operating room, but for a very different kind of patient.

"Hey Richards, wake the fuck up," she said as she stretched. "You're gonna get a needle in the ass!" The man didn't move—he hardly even seemed to be breathing.

Pike laughed. "I got this, Sammy. Wakey wakey, Richie," he said as he reached back into the truck cabin. He grabbed Richards by the shoulder and shook him, hard. The man stirred and his eyes slid open.

"Time to see the aliens, Richie!" Samantha wasn't about to let him live that one down. It was just too good to pass up.

Richards ignored her, but turned to face Pike, who was leaning in the doorway and grinning like an idiot. Samantha snickered—she'd discovered a new appreciation for the lumpy little man. Richards was all work all the time, but Pike was somebody you could talk to. At least the day hadn't been a complete disaster—she knew somebody who had been there and understood what they'd gone through.

"Come on Richie, no more sleeping on the job. Chop chop!" Pike clapped the back of his hand into his palm. Richards reached out and grasped the steering wheel—the motion was slow and aimless. "You can do better than that. Do I need to go back in there?"

A deep growl emanated from Richards' throat; the low rumble seemed to vibrate the walls within the quiet garage. Samantha's head snapped toward Richards, the hairs on the back of her neck at attention.

"Get a grip, Richie!" she said, pushing all her strength and anger into her voice. Fatigue gnawed at her joints and bones; she didn't have the benefit of napping all the way home, like he had. Her sunburned arms and neck fared little better—roasting as though her skin had become as radiant as the sun.

With a howl, Richards suddenly flung himself from the truck in one smooth, feral motion. He moved faster than Samantha thought was possible, and with a deadly purpose—he slammed into Pike's round gut and they both tumbled to the ground in a tangle of limbs. The men writhed, both trying to gain the advantage.

"Get off!" Pike had Richards by the throat, pushing the man's contorted mess of features away from his own. Richards' usually expressionless visage was twisted with a wild animalistic expression—teeth barred and eyes wide open.

Samantha looked to the tools behind her and grasped the longest one she could find, a long crowbar. It was heavy and the cold, scratched steel pressed into her palm. Almost five feet and weighing about twenty pounds, it was a formidable weapon. She swallowed once, and mapped out the quickest route to get to Pike. She ran to the other side of the truck, weaving through tools and hanging wires on her way. "Stop fucking around Richards!" she yelled as she rammed a glancing blow off his shoulder.

"Fuck!" Pike screamed as he pushed against Richards' weight. The man wasn't heavy, but he had much longer limbs than stumpy Pike, and he was relentless in pressing home his attack. The man's face was within an inch of Pike's throat, and his hands clawed at Pike's rumpled uniform.

Samantha clenched her teeth and swung the crowbar against Richards' exposed flank as hard as she could. The sickening crack of breaking bones filled the air and its reverberation travelled up the metal shaft into her hands. Richards shrieked; it was the same chilling and inhuman sound the rioters had made. But this time, it was not on some random crazed civilian, but one of their own, a man who had sworn an oath, and one she knew hadn't consumed any drugs. It was unfathomable, insane.

The instinct for survival took over, and she renewed her attack, striking at Richards' head, hip and even one of his arms that still held fast to Pike. The pain he should have felt didn't register, and the assault on Pike continued unabated. Her attacks were met with the same incessant screeching he'd presented before. His exposed skin was welted and bleeding, his scalp torn from his skull. It was as though she was smashing a piñata, rather than a human being. The crowbar was coated with gore, torn hair and flesh, grotesque in its absurdity.

Her tactic wasn't working, so she adjusted her hold and readied the crowbar like a lance. Pike and Richards were deadlocked. Pike's stubby hands were locked in a death grip around the other man's slim throat. Richards struggled to grab Pike's uniform, but Pike was always one step ahead in dodging the other's grasp.

She thrust the crowbar forward and there was a violent jolt as she hit her mark—the place where she had previously broken Richards' ribs. The crowbar met little resistance as it slid into his chest cavity. She twisted, attempting to skewer him and force him to yield his crazed attack. Blood and gore oozed down the shaft as she adjusted her angle, and Richards screamed—an agonized sound that was accompanied by a spray of blood from his mouth. Samantha couldn't imagine the degree of pain she'd inflicted on Richards, but she couldn't conceive how he managed to renew his attack, and with the same fervor as he'd possessed in the beginning.

With panic threatening to overtake her, Samantha pulled loose her makeshift javelin and centered herself on a new target—Richards' head. Kill the brain and the body would die. She hoped at least that small bit of wisdom still functioned in this crazy, messed-up world she found herself in. Her arms ached with the exertion of wielding such an unusual weapon, and Pike's shaking arms told her that his own strength was waning. He had forced his eyes and mouth closed against the fresh tide of blood that Richards spewed at him.

She thrust, and hit home. The steel bar broke through Richards' temple with surprising ease. She held her breath as she pushed harder, continuing until the crowbar's sharp end poked out the other side of his head. Richards went still then, but his muscles seemed only to be frozen, not slack with death's embrace.

The door burst open, and a group of armed men stormed into the garage. Relief flooded through Samantha, along with a twinge of fear. The men rushed over, with Captain McIntyre following close behind. His face was tightly controlled; his infectious smile now only a memory carved into the lines of his face. Samantha's arms strained as Pike wrestled his way out from beneath Richards' unmoving weight. She let her arms relax once Pike was free, and dropped her gruesome trophy to the floor, its point still lodged in Richards' skull. She stood at attention and waited for Captain McIntyre to speak. Part of her wanted to run away and hide from the frightening intensity of his piercing dark eyes, but she was no coward and stood her ground.

Remus didn't get a chance to speak—Richards leapt back to life with an ear-piercing howl, oblivious to the crowbar that was still lodged through his skull. He pushed himself to his feet, the bar hanging from his head at a sickening angle. Despite the protests of her aching and exhausted arms, Samantha rushed to seize hold of the end, just as one of the other soldiers drew his gun and fired two well-placed shots into the bloody mess that was Richards' head. Richards slumped to the ground; his ruined skull was a mess of bone and brains. Samantha forced the rising bile back down her throat—she'd seen death before, it was just another part of the job. But the dead were supposed to stay dead—especially corpses with crowbars impaling their skulls. She overcame both the conflicting urges that danced through her psyche. One was to run away and hide, and the other was to nudge the corpse with her boot. Part of her wanted to wake up and have all she'd been through be nothing more than a nightmare, but the other wanted to take the flamethrower and cook the monstrous bastards herself.

Pike stood next to her, but a little behind, as though he were trying to use her to shield himself from another attack. The blood on his face had become smeared with sweat and the rivulets had dried into repulsive brown streaks. The smell of blood permeated the air, but Samantha had grown used to it on the long drive back to the base. She squared her shoulders and looked hard at the men before her.

"Get me a sanitation team." Captain McIntyre barked the order to the stout man standing to his right, who nodded his acknowledgement and rushed out of the room. Once the man had left the building, McIntyre continued: "Tell me what happened."

"Well, I went to wake him up, and then he turned into one of those things from the city, Captain." Pike's explanation was short and to the point.

"Did you have any contact with them?"

"We were ambushed while we were laying down the Cemfoam on Heaven's Highway, Captain." Samantha spoke up. She knew the captain valued truth and honesty.

As a small team of men in white biohazard suits burst into the room, Remus cast one last look down at the bloodied thing that had been Richards. "Let's continue this elsewhere. I want you both decontaminated. I don't want a repeat of this incident."

"What about the other teams, Captain?" Samantha asked, unsure of how to broach the question.

"None of them made it back, Sammy."

Samantha stopped her just as her knees buckled. The other teams had more people, and better equipment. How could so many well-trained people have failed?

A dread chill crept up her spine as they stepped out into the muggy June night. There was nothing she could think to do, but she had faith that Remus had a plan. If he couldn't save the day, who else would?

Chapter 7

Samantha's sunburn raged under the pressure of the decontamination shower. The room's sterile stainless steel interior was only interrupted by a garbage chute hatch to the main incinerator and a closed door with a small slot that she presumed was for towel service. At least, she hoped it was for towel service—she'd already dropped her clothes into the incinerator chute and she didn't relish the idea of stepping out of the room buck naked. Her sunburn was an agony she could not become accustomed to. Most pains could be tolerated, or endured, but her searing skin being blasted by piping hot water and disinfectant solution was more than she could bear. Her inner turmoil lent no comfort to her predicament—killing Richards had been the most extreme action she had ever taken in defense of another. Her work was usually impersonal, clinical in nature, but Richards had been a colleague, if not a friend. On some level, she was able to understand the brutality of the events of the afternoon on Heaven's Highway, but Richards' transformation from a normal human being to slathering monster deeply disturbed her. She knew for a fact that he hadn't taken any drugs. Now, Captain

McIntyre was waiting in the next room; the man expected answers, and she had little to offer him.

After what seemed an eternity of resisting the need to writhe on the floor of the decontamination room, the intense shower finally relented. The smell of the acrid solution burned her throat and nose, and she reached for the towel that slid through the slot. She patted her angry red skin, wincing at every inadvertent brush of the abrasive fabric against her more sensitive spots. She noted that bruises had begun to form along her inner arms, which were already becoming tender and sore to the touch. She hoped she could replace her lost uniform, or at least her boots. She sighed and wrapped the towel around herself. She'd endured enough public humiliation in high school over her size, and felt no need to revisit the experience in front of her commanding officer.

Samantha stepped into the bright, unrelenting lights of the medical building. The light in the other decontamination chamber was still on—Pike was still enduring his own forceful cleansing. Clutching the towel against her, she scanned the room, and found that it was empty. It seemed like just another day on the base; no soldiers occupied the beds and the chief medic sat at a desk in the corner. Samantha looked around. Captain McIntyre was nowhere to be seen.

She approached the medic's desk. The man switched off his monitor before she was close enough to read what was on it, and stood. "Good, you're done. Please put on the gown," he said, gesturing to a small metal table just to the side of one of the other desks. A folded blue gown sat in the middle, its dull shades in stark contrast to the reflective luster of the metal.

Samantha moved to comply. All she wanted right now was a hot meal—even lukewarm gruel would be welcome at this point. Her stomach growled in defiance of her fear and disgust. She took small comfort in the biological imperative. Life must go on, no matter how twisted and disturbed it became. She managed to wiggle into the gown without dropping the towel. It was a skill she had mastered in gym class, being able to change while revealing nothing. Its light fabric was like a cool breeze against her savaged skin.

"She's ready." The medic spoke into an intercom, and the door opened. Two heavily armed men walked into the room.

"Come with us, Corporal Henderson. The Captain wants to see you," the man said, his face obscured by a tinted black visor. The other man was dressed similarly, but did not speak.

"Yes, Sir." She moved toward them, falling in formation between them as they exited the medical wing. Samantha was unaccustomed to walking barefoot, so she found the cool tile floor hard against her heels. Her right hand held the open back of the gown closed over her more compromising parts, but heat rose in her cheeks as the soldiers looked her over.

They came to their destination—the brig. Samantha tried to mask a stumble. She'd done nothing wrong! Nudged forward, she walked through the doors.

The brig was packed—almost every cell housed a single individual. Her escort opened one of the empty cell doors and motioned her inside. When she stepped in, the door slammed shut behind her. She pushed away the myriad emotions that threatened to overtake her. She felt betrayed. She'd acted in self-defense, and saved Pike's life. She shivered in the chilly air conditioned space as the transparent unbreakable metal barrier slid down to complete her incarceration. Sounds were drowned out, leaving her to listen to only the shaky quavering of her own breaths.

Samantha sagged onto the padded bench, fervently hoping that she would be offered the opportunity to redeem herself.

***

Samantha felt her bottom begin to grow numb as she luxuriated on the cold steel bench; she shifted her weight once again and leaned back as she continued to watch the guards move up and down the row. The patrols were methodical and punctual. Samantha figured she could set a clock by them and she found their efficiency curiously comforting, even sitting alone in a holding cell with no company but the ghosts of her past.

There was a flurry of activity at the empty cell directly across from hers. The guards were escorting a lumpy little man dressed, as she was, in only a hospital gown into the cell—it was Pike! Her heart jumped in momentary elation, but was just as quick to sink with the realization that he was being held captive, just as she was. But his imprisonment made no sense to her at all; he'd done nothing except defend himself against an attack by Richards. She had been the one who had killed his assailant. She couldn't help shuddering, again. At least the decontamination shower had scoured the stench of blood from her skin and hair. But nothing could erase the scent of death from her memory, or dull the horrific screams of the damned who had been exterminated. Those sensations would be far less transitive than mere dirt and grime. She looked over her hands, noting the chewed fingernails and blistering sunburn. Her eyes snapped shut for an instant.

She watched Pike through the clear metal sheet as he paced the length of his cell. She knew that the unbreakable, clear metal could turn black in an instant, blocking out all light to her. She doubted that she would be put in isolation, but she was not prepared to make any assumptions after the events of the previous day. Invading aliens, real-life zombies, skewering her colleague's skull with a crowbar—it was all just too much to process.

Samantha shifted again and then stretched her full length along the bench. Its design was painfully biased toward the smaller end of the height spectrum, and her bare feet dangled over the edge of the hard surface. She shivered against the chill of the cold metal, longing for a simple blanket to relieve her discomfort. She compromised by pulling her knees to her chest and hugging her shins to keep the warmth in. She closed her eyes and used all the mental tactics she knew to force her frenetic mind into a state of calm. Then, she surrendered herself to fatigue.

Chapter 8

Samantha's eyes slid open. Her first reaction was to test her muscles and skin, which burned with renewed fire. Then she noticed a group of grey-uniformed people standing in the corridor outside her cell. She thrust herself into a seated position, unwilling to be seen by her peers huddling in a fetal ball like an animal. The group moved away then, leaving Pike's cell across the hall empty. Samantha sighed, but her disappointment was tempered by the realization that Pike, at least, had been set free.

She stood, pulling her arms over her head, as she approached the impenetrable metal barrier for the first time. Her line of sight wasn't terribly good, but she was able to determine that the cells across from hers were empty. Though the guards were nowhere to be seen, jailbreak was all but impossible. Nothing audible had worked its way past the soundproof barrier, which gave the cell block an eerie, abandoned ambiance. Her heartbeat echoed through her ears and her breaths took on the hollow cadence of Darth Vader. At least, she thought his name was Darth Vader. Twentieth century movies weren't her strong point.

At last, a figure stepped into view. It was Captain McIntyre—he hadn't forgotten her! Samantha stood her ground as he nodded at the accompanying guard and the barrier began to rise into the ceiling. Noises and sounds rushed into her little cave, creating a cacophony of sensation. Her head spun for a moment, but she rushed to center herself. A tang of smoke tinged the air, but it could have been a remembered smell from the day before, or a waft of scent from a soldier's clothing. Samantha stood with as much dignity as her current dress would afford, and waited for him to speak.

"Okay Sammy, you're clean. Come with me and we'll get you some fresh clothes, then I need to hear everything," he said. Heavy bags weighed down his eyes, and his voice was hoarse and ragged. It seemed that she'd been afforded yet another luxury he denied himself—sleep.

"Yes, Sir." Samantha responded, eager to get out of the gown and into uniform once again.

They walked in silence to the administration center. McIntyre's office was small, but functional. A large wooden desk dominated one wall, along with medal display cases and certificates. Otherwise, the room was bare and utilitarian, lacking any stamp of individuality. A scattering of papers and a work tablet littered the desk. Usually, Remus was more fastidious. On the chair that faced the desk, there was a folded uniform and pair of boots.

"Take those and report back once you're dressed. We have some work to do." Captain McIntyre said as he crossed the room and sat in his chair. When he sank in his chair, she noted that his tired features seemed to have softened somewhat, perhaps by relief. Samantha grabbed the clothes and hurried as quickly as her bare feet could take her down the hall to the closest washroom.

Within the confines of the stall, under the harsh judgment of fluorescent lighting, Samantha examined the uniform. It was identical in size and style to her old one. The pressed fabric felt familiar and comfortable against her skin. She pushed her feet into the unyielding leather of her new boots, dreading the task of breaking them in, which seemed a pretty petty concern compared to everything that was going on. Then Samantha checked her hair, using a bit of water from the tap to spike her pixie cut back into shape. There were dark bags under her eyes and her cheeks and the bridge of her nose were red and raw from the peeling that had already begun. There was little she could do about that. On her way back to the captain's office, the thud of her new boots echoed down the empty hallway, restoring the trusted aura of power and strength that she strove to maintain despite the confusion and exhaustion of the past day's events.

She knocked on the side of the open door to signal her return. Remus looked up and motioned her to the empty chair. She sat down, biting the inside of her cheek to keep some semblance of a controlled exterior. She folded her hands on her lap and waited.

"I'm sorry I had to put you in quarantine last night, Sammy. But, I had to be sure you weren't..." he began, before his voice trailed off. He caught himself mid-pause, and continued: "one of *them*." The intonation on the word was so grave that it sounded like a different voice had spoken it.

"I understand, Sir." She didn't know what else to say. General acknowledgement was usually the best way to deal with superiors.

"I should have kept you in there for another day, but I need every soldier I can get. We've lost many good people in the past day alone, and the situation keeps getting worse. You're the only person who survived the mission to seal off the city, and I need to know what you saw." His words were measured and practiced, as though he'd spoken them in front of a mirror while she had been changing.

"Pike made it back, too," she offered, wishing her friend were there with her, so they could shoulder the burden of the debriefing together.

"Pike didn't make it, Sammy." His formerly vibrant brown eyes now looked dead and empty.

"But, he was fine before I went to sleep. I saw him in the cell across from me!"

"He turned into one of those ... *things* while you slept. We were forced to... eliminate him."

"I understand, Sir." Her eyes turned towards the floor. There was nothing else to say. The shock of the loss robbed her of her capacity to speak. She wanted to say something about what a good man and a good soldier he was, but nothing would surface through the despair she fought to keep from overpowering her. She remembered the smell of smoke in the air of the cell block. How many more had they exterminated as she slept behind that soundproof barrier?

"He's not alone. We've lost twenty percent of our standing force in one day, and that number doesn't include the many people still locked in quarantine cells. I need you to tell me everything and anything, even something that seems irrelevant. My job now is to write a report to Cartwright and the others. We need to let the other bases know what we're up against." His raptor gaze held her eyes, but his voice was soft and quiet. There was a real sorrow in it; their harrowing situation had distressed him to the depths of his soul. She knew that he had administrated this base for over a decade, and he knew everyone. They were the only family he had ever allowed himself.

"I'll tell you everything I know, Captain. I hope it helps and we can all stop this, together, as a team." At that moment, Samantha resolved to do everything in her power to make things right. She might not be able to bring back the dead, or heal the lost ones, but she could talk about what she saw, and maybe make a difference in the end. She paused for a moment; the events burned into her mind were so surreal that they called into question her sanity, and her integrity.

"Start from the beginning, Sammy. It's alright, you can talk to me. Then, we'll fix it. You'll see." The captain smiled, and his grey eyes were laced with the creases of empathy and concern. He pulled an old-style pen and paper out of his desk drawer. "Let's get started."

Samantha took a deep breath and began telling the haunting story of her last mission: the Cemfoam, the crazies, and the aliens. She could hardly believe it, herself. Her stomach knotted against itself as she spoke, and at times her voice failed her completely. Remus only nodded, and urged her to take her time. Her courage renewed, she would continue, thankful for the understanding she was receiving from her commanding officer.

***

Samantha dug into her meal, grateful for this reprieve from the day's grueling events. Her debriefing had taken almost four hours. The captain had picked apart every piece of the previous day's events, and had dragged her to the limits of her memory and mental endurance. The poor sleep she'd had in the holding cell the previous day had caused aches and exhaustion to settle deep into her bones. Only the persistent gnawing emptiness, coupled with the weakness in her limbs had prompted her to eat at all. The bland food rolled off her tongue, and her mind reeled from the day's events. She fought to hide her shaking hands, with limited success, by hiding them under the table as she chewed.

The mess hall was quiet, and the giant room seemed far too big for the small compliment of soldiers who sat hunched over their food. Entire tables were empty, and the scattered men and women who remained were sullen and quiet. Samantha saw weary grey faces mechanically chewing food, all eyes focused squarely on their plates. Her usual meal-time comrades and friends were nowhere to be seen, and she couldn't help but fear the worst.

Samantha tried to force down another mouthful, but found her throat refusing to respond. She set down her fork, moved to the bin and emptied the tray of its uneaten remains. Her eyes moved over the room, over the drained faces of the people sitting there.

She hung her head and began the walk back to her room in the barracks. She hoped that the drills Captain McIntyre had scheduled for her tomorrow would clear her mind, and bring back her sense of security and normalcy.

For now, all she wanted to do was lose herself in sleep.

Chapter 9

"And we will take back our countryside by whatever means necessary. We have sacrificed so much, but we must maintain the peace until we can get reinforcements. We will hold this land for the nation... keep our people safe and maintain the rule of law until the government gives us new orders."

"We will keep this place clear and free of the marauding enemy. Who is with me?" Captain McIntyre's voice resounded within the belly of the mess hall. Most of their once two-thousand strong force could now fit in the room that had once required several rotations to serve all the souls who served there. Only the medics and the contingents of guards who patrolled the ancient stone wall perimeter were not in attendance. The assembly had been mandatory for all other staff.

The crowd erupted into cheers, as infectious as they were hopeful. Some beat their fists against the tables, other stood and clapped. Samantha sat in silence, her eyes turned to the captain, who stood basking in the hope and change he envisioned. She knew he could do it, and she was going to do everything in her power to help him.

"Thank you, thank you," the man continued, hanging his head and spreading his arms. "We are a family, and families help each other. We're going to take care of each other, and the people under our protection. In the next few days, we'll be starting a new offensive, one that will turn the tide in our favor. Eat well, train hard and be strong. We have great things to do, and our people will be safe because of our courage and sacrifice. Now rest up, because we have a hard road ahead of us. " With that, he walked out of the room, flanked by his two aides. They were a new addition to his retinue; Samantha didn't remember them assisting him before. Perhaps the losses had included his previous personal assistants, as well. Samantha felt a bite of jealousy, but fought it down. She would have her chance to join his inner circle—she just needed to prove herself to be capable and trustworthy.

The room was awash in conversation, and Samantha found her mood lifting. She hadn't seen and of her friends or bunkmates in the three days since the chaos began. She'd inquired about their whereabouts, but found the information blocked at every turn. Casualty lists weren't being posted, and normally friendly and helpful clerks had become tight-lipped and withdrawn. When she went for her evening jog around the grounds, her eyes scanned for the three girls she'd met in basic training. They had been thrilled to find out that they'd all been assigned to the same posting. That was two years ago, but now it seemed Samantha had lived several lifetimes since then. Samantha wished she knew what had happened to them, where they had gone. She needed to hear their infectious laughter, wanted the simple joy of a girl's movie night, yearned for somebody to talk to who really cared.

Off hours were long. The television feed never worked, and most of the phones were monopolized by people trying to reach their families. Samantha had bought a call voucher for that evening—she wanted to call her brother, to make sure he was alright. She needed to know that somewhere, the world was still happy and sane … or at least as sane as modern Earth could be. Things had made more sense in the 2020s when she was growing up, until she'd realized how little opportunity there was for people like her. That was before she'd lost her parents and all hope for the future with them. The Peacemakers had become a bandage over the sense of hopelessness that bathed her future, but she knew her career there would eventually come to an end. After that, she didn't know what she'd do. College was restricted to the chosen few, and trade schools had five year waiting lists. All she could do was save the bulk of each pay and hope to qualify for a promotion or supplemental training. Without her friends and family, the bleakness of her life could stretch until senility.

Samantha left the hall. She needed to take a long, sweaty run to clear her mind. The air outside was clear and fresh; there were no screams of pain or strife, only the late afternoon chatter of birds and wildlife. The overcast day was chilly for almost-July, and the cool air worked life back into her numbed senses. The old stone wall dominated the horizon, its stark grayness in contrast to the green of the trees beyond its confines, and the grass inside. She found herself running faster, as the seeds of doubt began to multiply in her mind once again. She seldom gave in to the hopelessness of her reality, the lost dreams of painting and drawing, talents that she could never invest the time to develop. She put down riots for a living, riots caused by the same pervasive futility that had snuffed out her family's dreams. But, what could she do? Compliance and riot control were the only branches of the army where genetic amplification wasn't a requirement, and Samantha couldn't quite shake her visceral revulsion toward the idea of being fundamentally and permanently changed, her cloned teeth notwithstanding. Would she still be herself afterward? Could she still paint, laugh and feel, the same as she did now? The new, hardened soldiers, the *altered* ones, were another breed: they didn't count pain, regret or despair as relevant. Only pride in their duty and an impressive set of rock-hard muscles mattered to them. Samantha possessed the latter, hard earned the old-fashioned way. She didn't want to lose what little of her own identity she had left; she didn't want to be dehumanized any further than she already had been. It was true that the army had taken away her fear and replaced it with solidarity and purpose, but she couldn't imagine having those attributes forcibly added to her genetic code. It was just wrong, though she would never publicly admit to that view. It was far safer to show a zeal for her current work, than to demean the heroes in every other field of service. Would her brother or lost parents even recognize her?

As she rounded the final corner in her run, she saw the iron gates open in the distance. A convoy of personnel carriers rolled into the base and the cheering and hollering that resounded in response to their arrival pulled Samantha from her wistful thoughts, back into reality. This must be the new initiative Captain McIntyre had spoken of. She's been so engrossed in drills and practice that she hadn't noticed the activities of the other squads. The drills had been grueling, brutal and mind-numbing—she'd barely noticed the passage of time, and other than her friends' conspicuous absences, the world had seemed to melt back into a state of regularity. The smell of Cemfoam clung to her clothes and hair even after washing.

As she turned back and headed toward the barracks, the cheering intensified, and horns blasted their strident commentary into the tranquil evening. It was time to call her brother; she would figure out what the celebration was about later.

Chapter 10

"Yeah, and we killed all those sons of bitches! The fire lit 'em up, and we watched them dance and scream in the flames. The bastards are going to regret ever fucking with us!" The young corporal spoke, his voice shaking with excitement. His pale blue eyes darted to the faces around the table, and Samantha found herself nodding. The protruding veins in his forehead and on the back of his hands, as well as his too-broad shoulders marked him as an augmented soldier. His narrow jaw and squeaky voice were in direct conflict with his physique. His skin was greyer than a normal person's—the gift of his new blood. He made the hairs on the back of Samantha's neck stand on end.

"Yeah, but how many of us were lost this time around?" asked a petite woman sitting to Samantha's right. Samantha had started to hang out with a new group during meals, to lessen the sting of the absence of her friends. Their names hadn't appeared on the list of casualties, which was last updated just over a week ago. To make matters worse, she had never been able to reach her brother. Her calls went directly to voicemail and her messages were never returned. Steve lived a thousand kilometers away, but she couldn't help wondering if the insanity had spread that far, so fast.

"None at all!" came the answer. "The captain is smart Mandy, smarter than those crazy sons-of-bitches will ever be! We burned 'em down, and the fuckers screamed until their throats melted." The man took another swig of water—water was the only drink still allowed, or available, on base. Samantha wasn't sure which, not anymore.

"Did you find any survivors?" Samantha asked, watching the man's prominent Adam's apple work up and down as he drank.

"You'd think they could give a man a beer after all that," he complained. "No survivors, why would there be any?" He shrugged.

"I don't know. Just hoping, I guess," Samantha said with a shrug, as she gazed down into her own glass of water.

"Come on, we're better off without that dead weight. They can take care of themselves. We're just here to keep the base secure, and take care of the strong. That's how we survive!"

"That doesn't sound like what I signed up for," Samantha replied, her eyes drifting to the clock. She contemplated finding new people to share her meals with.

"Come on, Henderson. You specialize in Compliance and Riot Control. You can't tell me you give a fuck what happens to people," the man spat, to which Mandy, the girl sitting next to Samantha, laughed.

"I care about protecting the people who can't protect themselves, and maintaining order. It's as simple as that." Samantha stated, glowering; she didn't like having her motives for signing up questioned.

"A fucking idealist, just what we need. Well, you'll get called one day, and we'll see who needs *protection* then." The man shot her a glare and stood to leave. Then Mandy rolled her eyes and stood up, slamming her chair into the table.

"I can't believe *she's* the only one who made it back on day zero. God sure has a sense of humor." Mandy's voice trailed into the background. Samantha's face grew hot, and she chugged the rest of her water to cool the flush in her cheeks. God had nothing to do with her escape. Luck, training, and quick thinking had, coupled with a tank of Cemfoam.

Samantha sighed. She missed her old friends, their understanding and especially their ability to remain grounded in what really mattered.

Mandy's chair was pulled out, and Captain McIntyre sat down next to her. "Captain!" she said, her eyes widening, as the bustling sounds of the mess hall grew distant. Could he have overheard the argument?

"That's me. And, for the record, I can believe that you were the only one to survive. How are you holding up, Sammy? I thought I should check in. I heard you were looking for some of your missing friends."

"Yes, Sir. I never saw them again after day zero, but they're not on any of the lists," Samantha said, her voice quiet against the noisy backdrop.

"This is a hard time for all of us. The casualty lists are still being updated, but it's hard to spare the manpower to make sure everything is accurate, or complete. Since the internet went down, most of our computers are useless terminals. The clerks have been doing things by hand, between drills. I will have it looked into for you, I promise Sammy." His smile warmed her heart, but not his grey eyes. They were tinted with another emotion, and seemed to burn with an intensity not granted to most humans.

"Are there survivors?" Samantha had to know, she couldn't accept that they were killing the enemy, at the cost of neglecting the civilians under their protection.

"Of course, we're doing everything we can for them, but we need to keep a fifty mile perimeter around this base safe. How can we protect them if the enemy can simply walk up to our gates? Remember Mrs. Tyler and her summer school classes? They're here, safe in the unused storage areas and yards—you can take your evening jog that way tonight and say hello. We can do that for so many more people, Sammy; we just need to keep it secure, keep the civilians and their children out of harm's way. And, we need to be able to feed them." His raptor gaze held her eye, but a speck of doubt still lingered inside her, coiled around her heart.

"Thank you for clearing that up for me, Sir. Was there something else you wanted to talk to me about?" Samantha chose not to give voice to her fears, afraid they might betray her. She admired the Captain, and didn't want him to think less of her. She knew he would always do the right thing, and it wasn't her place to question him.

"I want you on the next outgoing team, to secure the town of Pennington. Do you think you're ready to return to active duty?" His eyes scanned the crowd as he talked.

"I hadn't realized I was off active duty, Captain. I'm too tired at night to be taking it easy," Samantha said, glancing back to the clock.

"I wanted to make sure you're one of us. I won't put my people in harm's way if I can help it. You've fought those things, so I'm sure you understand the necessity of taking precautions."

"Yes, Sir." Samantha didn't understand how she could be converted to one of them. None had laid a hand on her. There must be something else to it, something he wasn't telling her. The faces of Richards and Pike flashed in her mind for an instant. She blinked to force them back to the black place they'd come from.

"You'll get your orders later. There are a lot of opportunities with this organization now, Sammy. Do good by your squad leaders and you'll get noticed. You've got a head on your shoulders, so make sure you use it." Captain McIntyre patted her on the back as he stood up and then he left as quickly as he'd come, leaving her staring at the clock.

She would get her chance now. She knew it. She stared at the clock as the butterflies began a slow flutter in her stomach. She couldn't mess this up.

Chapter 11

The bumpy roads rocked the cramped personnel carrier from side to side, and Samantha was worried that she'd succumb to a bout of motion sickness before she arrived at their destination. She found it interesting that this was the first time she'd experienced motion sickness since enlisting; she'd thought that the uncomfortable and often embarrassing condition was long behind her. To distract herself from her growing discomfort, she scanned her surroundings. The faces around her were all young, but their faces and bodies displayed the kind of weariness she'd only seen in older servicemen, like Richards or Pike. Samantha hoped she would never grow that old—in that regard, she held the captain as a role model; life's troubles seldom seemed to touch the man, and he could offer up a smile in almost any situation.

The group was silent. Samantha recognized the man she and Mandy had eaten dinner with the day before—his name was Biggs. He'd fixed her with a hard glare the moment he took his seat near the doors, and had made a point of ignoring her ever since. Samantha was more than happy to accommodate him. She didn't want to get chummy with glory-seeking super soldiers. To her, it was just a job, and her duty was to protect innocent lives. Samantha figured Biggs may have signed up for the wrong line of work; he certainly didn't belong in hers. He belonged on the front lines of the latest resource war, or keeping dissenters from slipping across the border to freedom.

They'd been sealed in the hot, stuffy compartment for just over an hour. The cloying stench of fresh sweat clung to what little air remained, serving only to heighten the queasiness Samantha's already sour stomach. She just wanted to get her feet on the ground, do her job and go back home knowing that because of her effort, the world was a better place. If there was still a world left. Why didn't Steve call her back?

She sighed as the vehicle slowed to a stop; her head spinning from the combination of motion sickness and heat. She gripped her seatbelt and took a deep, shaking breath. She didn't want to leave the safe confines of the carrier, but she knew she had to. Captain McIntyre was counting on her—if he believed in her, how could she doubt herself?

She moved from the carrier as though she was suspended in a dream—the bright, early-morning July sun blinded her. She blinked to center herself. In her hands, she held a weapon and a riot shield. The shield gave her a grounded sense of safety that came from countless hours of exercises and drills. She holstered the gun and took up her position. Captain McIntyre had adapted their crowd control training to excel at containing masses of the infected. They were ancient techniques, but they'd held off wave after wave of the attackers, leaving them exposed to the powerful flamethrowers were being assembled. It was a brilliant strategy, but she could sense the trepidation in the quiet obedience of her peers. She didn't relish watching people burn to death, but no other way had been found to stop their advance, and she wasn't about to volunteer to mediate.

Her eyes scanned the scene in front of her as she stood shoulder-to-shoulder with her peers. Pennington was a tiny village by all accounts, home to about one hundred people. Crows clung to the dilapidated rooftops of the row of two-story homes worn away by neglect and age. The cracked street was interspersed with potholes, and corpses. A pair of mangled bodies lay about a block down the street, their brown blood tarring the faded pavement. An army of flies danced over the corpses, laying their eggs in the human pulp. The smell of rot hung heavy in the air.

Another smell began to engulf the stench of decay: that of Cemfoam being deployed behind their line. The expectation of bloodshed rose in her throat with bitter bile as she imagined the gruesome deaths playing out on the stage before them. She swallowed and refocused her concentration. The plan was simple: she and the majority of the squad would shield the makeshift corral until the Cemfoam was deployed, then they would make noise to draw out the fiends. If all went as planned, the things would run straight into an ambush and be unable to evade the searing liquid death that awaited them. Samantha didn't relish the idea of being part of the bait, but she'd faced this enemy before, and while they were bloodthirsty and ruthless, the concept of strategy was lost on them.

The tingling in her sinuses only increased as the Cemfoam set, and Samantha stood still and silent, her weapon at the ready. She skimmed the rows of houses and bodies in anticipation of being the first to spot the movement of one of the restless ghouls who threatened the safety of all who lived nearby. She wiped her sweaty palms on her pants leg and shifted her weight from foot to foot, never taking her eyes from the landscape, and using her peripheral vision to gauge the behavior of the men who stood on either side of her. The sun became hotter as it continued its ascent, and Samantha's fair skin stung with the combination of sunburn and sweat. Her personal supply of sunscreen had run out four days ago, and there was none to be found on base.

A hand reached out and tapped her left shoulder twice—that was the signal. She did the same to the man on her left, before turning and walking into the structure of newly-set Cemfoam. With enough training and time, Cemfoam could be coaxed into structures over two meters in height, and the engineers could even enhance the structure with small windows, designed to fire through. Samantha angled herself through the narrow entrance, and took her position at the window to the far left. They'd created a T-shaped structure, a kind of mobile bunker that was always used as a theoretical model of what Cemfoam could do, rather than an actual combat structure. Until recently, that is. With a few modifications, the final certification test for advanced combat engineers had become a twenty-minutes-to-deploy trap for zombies. She waited, peering out the small window, the cool relief of shade overpowered by the nervous churning of her gut.

A man in a loose-fitting fire-retardant suit stepped in front of their makeshift bunker, his face totally obscured by a heavy mask. His name was Sanchez—the man who put down the raging masses. While Samantha had gained a certain notoriety as the only person who'd come back from sealing the major roadways of the capital, Sanchez had become famous for the unrelenting destruction meted out by his weapon. His hands held the flamethrower that had ended so many conflicts like this one. The soldier to her right muttered a quiet prayer, sending a shiver down her spine. Samantha sucked in a deep breath and exhaled, repeating the calming pattern she'd learned at a summer camp so long ago. A heightened awareness settled into her as Sanchez let out a mighty bellow, followed by the jeers and howls of her comrades. She was swept up in their zeal, hollering and screaming her taunts into the empty, dead streets.

Moments later, the streets came to frightful life with the distorted growls and shrieks that answered back. "Get ready!" Sanchez bellowed back at them, his voice almost drowned out by the cacophony. Samantha's eyes widened as she scanned the perimeter. If all went as planned, she wouldn't even need to fire a shot. If not, they'd be taking the heat—and blasting the enraged monsters off Sanchez. She swallowed a few more times, and consciously slowed her breathing to maintain its meditative pace.

A pair of the walking dead rounded the corner—two women. They wore the tattered remnants of floral sundresses, the stained fabric swaying in the breeze. Samantha caught herself smiling, just before the throng of about ten followed behind them. As her eyes scanned each bloody, tattered body, her mind was taken back to her time at the school, the crunch of crisped bone under tires and the smell of scorched hair and flesh tainting the summer air. This time, it was easier to believe they truly were the enemy, not just helpless civilians caught up in the chaos. Their bodies were leaner, more feral, and their faces angular, with greying skin stretched across the facial bones. Hair was clumped in thinning patches across their heads, and their deathly pallor seemed unaffected by the sun's intense heat.

The things didn't even look human anymore. Samantha wanted to open fire, to eradicate their toothy scowls from the face of the Earth with a salvo of hot lead. She steeled herself against this impulse, staying true to her orders. Instead, she looked to Sanchez, observing the ease of his posture, alone against the horde. His stance widened; then he cocked the weapon in front of him and unleashed a short burst of flame.

The heat rolled over Samantha in an instant, its power biting into her already sun-blistered skin. The approaching horde continued their frenzied charge. One by one, her comrades fell silent. The only remaining sound was the howling clamor of the angry wretches that were coming straight for them.

Without warning, fire erupted from the nozzle, flowing with a relentless purpose toward the incoming attackers. As the lapping flames embraced their limbs, their vocalizations turned agonized and desperate as they collapsed into a sizzling heap of flesh and bone. The air filled with the meaty stench of burning flesh mixed with the acrid bite of burnt hair and clothing. Samantha's nostrils twitched as she blinked away the soot and ash that billowed from the crisping bodies. For each monster that fell, more surged forward to take their place, all of them crowding in around Sanchez. He dispatched them one cluster at a time, their bodies flailing in a terrifying dance of death as the flames rolled through.

The flow of bodies slowed. Eventually, all that remained was a jumble of smoldering corpses, some still twitching. The men around her cheered loudly, snapping Samantha out of the spell of death that gripped her and threatened to never let her blink again.

`Move out!" a voice bellowed, and she and the rest of the bait filed out of the enclosure.

Samantha couldn't help smiling as she gazed upon the squirming pile of death before her, cracking the dry skin that stretched across her face in the process. It was time to go shopping.

***

Samantha perused the local pharmacy's selection of sunscreen, trying to decide if she should just take one bottle or two, or dump the entire shelf's contents into her bag. She'd already taken as many dental hygiene products as her simple backpack would allow, and she'd also claimed a generous selection of soap and shampoo. A good shower was just the thing everyone back on base needed. It was a cozy small-town pharmacy, offering just the essentials in personal care products. Fortunately, the establishment had been left untouched by looters. For good measure, she selected an assortment of the highest-SPF sunscreen available. She never tanned, so her only concern was avoiding more sunburns this summer. Samantha suspected that it would be a while before any cancer-removal clinics were back in business. If only sunscreen could protect the skin from the harsh heat of flamethrowers as well.

Samantha was contemplating the virtues of a new moisturizing cream for her singed skin when she heard a commotion outside. Moments later, she heard a woman's sobs echoing through the empty aisles. Samantha set down her half-full bag and moved toward the front of the store.

"Where are you? Are you hurt?" Samantha asked, following the cries. The sound was plaintive, a sharp contrast to the howls and screams of the damned.

"I—" the voice began, before being silenced by a hail of gunfire.

"No!" Samantha screamed, charging out of the building. What she saw when she got outside was the bullet-riddled body of an emaciated young woman still twitching on the ground. Samantha looked around with wild eyes, searching her surrounding to identify the person who had done this terrible thing.

"Bastards try to sneak up on you. There's always one or two left over after a burn," the fighter said, grinning down at his handiwork. She saw a square jaw, softened by the chubbiness of youth, and the barest shadow of stubble marring his clean appearance. She recognized him as one of the young soldiers who clung to Biggs and Mandy, the kind who needed bravado to shelter them from harsh reality. She'd eaten at the same table with him once or twice, but that's where the association ended.

She gazed down at the body, her heart still pounding in her chest. "Are you sure she was one of them?"

His dark eyes burrowed into her own pale blue, eyebrow cocked. "What, was she a fucking friend of yours or something?" he said, his tone full of sarcasm.

"No, but what if she was a survivor? What if she was one of the people we're here to protect?"

"Don't be so fucking green, Sammy. There are no survivors. The captain said it himself. Now just relax and get back to your tampon shopping." He turned from her then and drew radio out of his pocket: "I need a flamethrower in front of the pharmacy. Damn stragglers."

Samantha's face flushed a dark and painful red as she balled her hands into fists and marched back into the pharmacy.

This wasn't right. It wasn't right, at all.

Chapter 12

Biggs spoke from the cramped corner of their carrier. "Let Sammy do it; we need to be sure she's really on our side."

"You sure, Biggs? Sanchez gets the job done right." Mandy sneered as she spoke.

"You guys got a problem?" Samantha asked. She'd had enough of their innuendos.

"We think you need a second chance. Maybe we all got off on the wrong foot. So, how about you torch the next town full of those sons of bitches, and we'll see that you're not a spy for them? Sound good?"

"How could you possibly think I'm a spy? Those things don't even talk, in case you didn't fucking notice." Samantha spoke as she might to a small child.

"Nobody else came back, and then you go running around for days like the Captain's pet, worrying about survivors. It's too convenient. So, you give Sanchez a break and we reevaluate our opinions. Deal?" His grin overpowered his narrow jaw, but his eyes held a cold glint. Mandy snickered next to him.

"Maybe Sanchez can learn a thing or three from me. I'll do it." Samantha said confidently, noting with some pleasure that the smiles were quick to melt from their faces.

"Well, it's a good thing you'll fit his equipment." Mandy stuck her nose up as she spoke.

Bitch. "Anything else you want?" Samantha asked.

"We'll see once the next town is cleared, Sammy. Then we'll know how done I am with your hide."

Samantha only sighed in response. Then a rapid series of bumps jostled them around and diverted their attention to other things. She'd better convince them, or this posting was guaranteed to get a lot more unpleasant.

***

Samantha finished pulling on the heavy suit, grateful that the special gear would block the relentless mid-afternoon sun and the stench of Cemfoam. Her breath rumbled through her ears, reminding her of a pyromaniac version of Darth Vader. Again with Darth Vader—she'd even rewatched the original movies one evening, just to be sure. She doubted that even the tremendous power of the Force could lull the sickness in her stomach and the trembling of her knees. She didn't want to do this, but she needed to prove her loyalty to the others and have them leave her in peace. Her Peacemaker family had mutated into a pack of wolves. She was desperate to find a way to maintain her humanity, and not descend into the kind of beasts they had become.

Thoughts raced through her mind. What if the people that rushed toward her were really survivors? What if the flamethrower didn't work? What if there were just too many of them? What if these zombies were made of asbestos? She shook her head to clear away the uncertainty and noise. She had to do this.

Biggs nudged her from behind. That was her signal to get into position.

She checked her bindings and fuel line again, before taking examining the scene. They were boxed into a small parking lot enclave that sat between two buildings. The streets here, like with the last village, were in a sad state of disrepair, the dip between sidewalk and road had cracked open and become a mutated super-pothole. She craned her neck to check both sides of the enclosure—there were no point of access other than the streets. Few surprises would be coming her way.

Samantha took a step forward and let loose a test barrage with the flamethrower. Satisfied, she bellowed "Come get some!" into the empty air. She'd rehearsed that one in her mind, hoping the gusto of its delivery might grant her some needed credibility from her peers. She dropped her left foot back into a fighting stance and waited.

The people behind her erupted into a cacophony of taunts and jeers, their bloodlust shouted into the clear sky. They were hollering and screaming for blood. Samantha swallowed and steadied herself on her feet, willing her hands to stillness and opening herself to their collective bloodlust. She could do this. Her knees sank into a fighting stance, and her gloved hands squeezed against the handle of her newest weapon. She could smell Sanchez's body odor in the suit—she imagined it to be a benevolent spirit ready to help her on this latest labor.

The initial wave approached fast from the left, their gaunt grey skin torn and their soulless eyes wide. She held off on the impulse to fire. Timing was everything, she told herself, her heart whooshing loudly in her ears.

She kept a silent count of her breaths in her head, waiting until the screeching that assailed her ears became unbearable. Her finger tightened on the trigger and she loosed her first barrage of liquid death into the swarm. Their howls turned to agonized screams as they dropped to the ground, flames erupting over their limbs and bodies.

Time played tricks on her mind—sometimes everything seemed to be standing still, other times the writhing bodies seemed to blur passed her. The entire event merged into one long, horrific howl. Sweat dripped down her brow into her eyes. Her throat was unbearably dry. She gripped her weapon for dear life; it was all that shielded her against the frenzied masses, all that kept her alive and free from becoming one of them.

Samantha screamed into the mask and took a step forward, pressing her attack. Cheers erupted behind her, spurring her forward. A surge of energy continued to propel her forwards, and she looked around, dismayed that there were no enemies left to kill.

She pressed on, approaching the middle of the lot. One straggler sprinted around the corner, straight at her. It was a middle-aged woman, whose skin not yet having taken on the grey mask of not-quite death.

Samantha gritted her teeth and unleashed a new assault. The woman came to a dead halt and turned to shield herself from the flames. "No!" she screamed, before the flames enveloped her, replacing her plea with agonized screams.

Samantha's eyes widened. She dropped the weapon and bolted toward the woman. The innocent woman rolled on the ground in a futile attempt to extinguish the fire that feasted on her bubbling flesh. Samantha ripped off her protective gear and beat on the flames.

She can't die. I won't let her die! Samantha thought.

Samantha had managed to roll the woman over when a pair of hands hauled her away, and a single gun blast ended the victim's suffering. "Why?" Samantha screamed after she pried off the mask, turning to face her comrades.

"Get ahold of yourself, Sammy. It's just another zombie bitch," Biggs said, his mouth twisted downwards into a grimace.

"She was trying to run away! I saw it! Zombies don't run away!" Samantha spat the words through heaving breaths, tears stinging her eyes. This wasn't right. They were supposed to protect innocent people, not burn them alive.

"Fuck, Sammy. You were doing so well. Go on patrol; clear your mind. I'm sure you were just seeing things."

"I hope you're right." Samantha spoke barely above a whisper and walked back to the truck. She knew she was right, but the way things stood, she knew there was nothing she could do.

Chapter 13

The sun had already set by the time they arrived back at the base and the moon was a faint sliver in the sky. Samantha stared up at the stars a while and then set out on her evening jog. Her muscles and bones ached and her skin was blistered and singed in spite of the heavy protective suit she'd worn, but running was the only thing that could give her peace. She needed to purge the woman's anguished screams from her mind and find a way to accept the disturbing reality that she had likely murdered an innocent woman who simply needed help.

Samantha's body rebelled against the harsh pace she set, but she pressed forwards into the cooled nighttime air. The woman's cries bored through her awareness, so she picked up the pace, hoping to leave them far behind. The pleading brought up other ghosts from the past—her parents, her lost girlfriends, and even Richards and Pike appeared in her mind's eye.

Samantha was many things, and her line of work had often put her at odds with the civilian population she was tasked with protecting. But, she wasn't a murderer!

She stopped to catch her breath near the previously abandoned storage yards. A group of tents had been erected between the buildings and the smell of cooking food and campfire smoke permeated the air . She peered through the high chain-link fence and spied a large group of school-aged children sitting around a campfire. She couldn't see their faces, but their shoulders were slumped and their heads bowed toward the ground.

Samantha sighed, and began walking around the perimeter, her fingers trailing along the fence. They were safe, at least. But how many others were hiding in barricaded basements or cowering indoors, blinds drawn, without the benefit of walls, razor wire, and an entire militia surrounding them and keeping them safe? Samantha didn't want to contemplate the answer—the answer might be more than her wounded soul could handle.

The camp fire blazed, and Samantha found herself drawn to it. The pop and sizzle of the wood brought her back to her days at summer camp, and the happiness and simplicity of her childhood. Following a day of paddling a canoe or running through the trees, she enjoyed simply gazing into the inferno while the others sang along. It was strange how even after witnessing the terrifying destructiveness of fire earlier in the day, that she now felt drawn to its warmth, kinship and community.

Samantha hardly noticed the nibbling of mosquitos and flies as she looked out at the students. The desperate rescue operation in the school was now a fading memory, but she was proud of how she'd handled herself there. Because of her efforts, these kids were safe, fed and had a chance at a future. Maybe, like with her, not the future they dreamed of, but some kind of future anyway.

Samantha moved her hand to swat away a fly whose buzzing in her ear had drowned out the sounds of the bonfire.

"You're in my spot, Sammy," the Captain's voice said behind her.

Samantha jumped and turned around. "Sorry, Sir." She'd been so preoccupied, she hadn't even heard his approach. The fire's flickering still called to her, singing the sirens song of acceptance and brotherhood.

"At ease, Sammy. You've had a rough day," he said. The fire's light danced across his dark features as he continued. "This is where I come when I need to think, when I have tough decisions to make."

Samantha managed a smile. "It was nothing I couldn't handle, Captain," she said, looking away from him.

"You're a bad liar. I read Biggs' report. Don't worry about what happened today; I've dealt with Biggs." His eyes remained focused on the bonfire as he spoke. "Just keep on doing a good job, Sammy."

Samantha shuffled her feet. "It's more than that, Sir. I think ..." she began. But what could she tell him? That she'd killed an innocent, or that she showed compassion for the enemy. Both were wrong.

"There are no survivors, Sammy. How could anyone survive in a town full of those things? Think about it ... we know whatever this is, it spreads through just breathing the air for a long time. They'd be turned well before now. Don't be so hard on yourself. You did the right thing back there." He stretched his arm out and patted her on the shoulder.

She could feel the tension draining from her. "But, you said there were survivors yesterday; how can there be none today, Sir?"

"In more remote areas there are isolated families, mostly living in farm houses. But this isn't the case near population centers. You'll see when you go back on assignment tomorrow. We're going to secure another small town, and I want you to go with them. I know you can do this."

"I'll go wherever you send me, Captain." She didn't have any choice, but her father had always said: if you have to do something, you might as well enjoy it.

"Good. Check your posting on the screen in the barracks. We're fighting for these children, remember that. Someday this will all be over, and they'll be grown up and grateful for the sacrifices we made to make their world safe." Remus McIntyre smiled at her and then he turned on his heel and walked away, back in the direction of the Administration building.

Samantha only nodded. Her stomach was tying itself in knots once again. It wouldn't be over soon enough. She was grateful for a commanding officer who cared about the people under him, who took the time to reassure them in their new role—defending the future from the horde of undead.

Chapter 14

Samantha wiped the sweat that was beading on her nose. Once again, she and her comrades were enduring a bumpy ride in the personnel carrier, on their way to their first stop of the day. The village of Smith's Corners was their destination—the briefing had indicated that there was little of interest there, just a few small shops and an agricultural supplier. Regardless, Samantha willed her resolve to return.

Her eyes were heavy from lack of sleep, and the nightmares that visited her when she did sleep refused to fade. Always screaming, burning bodies would surround her, pointing fingers and cornering her in the dark recesses of a Cemfoam bunker. She'd awake in a cold sweat, unsure at first if it had been just a dream, or was a real memory. Sometimes, she'd seen her father charging headlong into the flames, hand-in-hand with her mother and brother.

She kept her eyes fixed on the floor. Biggs was seated across from her and she could feel his eyes boring into the top of her head. He hadn't acknowledged her when she'd first boarded the carrier, and Mandy had shot her an angry, disapproving look. No one spoke, and most everyone on board gave off the impression that they had discovered something fascinating on the floor, or some splotch marring the shine of their boots.

It was going to be a long day.

***

The ground crunched under Samantha's feet and the acrid smell of burnt bodies and Cemfoam assailed her nostrils once again. She'd been made to stay in the vehicle with the specialists and scavengers while the rest of the team had made short work of the zombie residents of the village. She was relieved to be out of the truck—she'd had to try so hard not to give the impression that she was affected by the howls and screams of the enemy, or the jeering taunts of the members of their militia.

She swallowed as she surveyed the scene—about three dozen charred bodies lay in the small parking lot, some still twitching. The flesh on one corpse's face had been completely burned away, revealing the grinning skull that lay underneath. The jaw held no front teeth and the dead eye sockets were filled with the cooked remnants of eyes. Samantha turned away, glancing into the gloom of the overcast sky.

"Good of you to join us, Henderson. How about you stand guard outside the feed store? You can make sure none of the zombies steal our farm equipment."

"Yes, Sir," she said, and then turned on her heel and marched off, leaving Biggs and his crew to their work.

***

The seed mill has an earthy musk hanging present in the air, a scent so strong that even the smell of death and fire could not challenge it. Samantha took in a round of cleansing breaths.

She paced in front of the mill, a wooden structure that had settled somewhat to the left side, leaving its wooden slats pressed against each other. The paint was peeling and the old style windows looked as though they might have been new when her grandparents were born. Samantha marveled that it was still standing. The mill was located on a dead end street. A field of corn stood opposite the entrance, the strong stalks of the plants leaned in the wind. At the end of the road was a grove of maple trees. Samantha was instantly reminded of the corn roasts she'd been to as a child, the smell of barbecue, and the memory of slick butter running down her chin. She allowed the pleasant recollection to linger as she imagined the taste of sweet corn slathered in butter. She wondered what would become of that field of corn, with no one left to tend it.

A rustling sound came from a bush at the side of the road, and Samantha moved to investigate. A quick check over her shoulder showed that Biggs was still standing in the doorway of the feed store, with his back to her. *Good*, she thought. *I want to investigate whatever it is before he does.*

She walked over and stooped down, weapon at the ready. Two pairs of eyes peered back at her, sunken into their small dirty faces. One was a girl of about nine or ten, the other a boy of six, but their gaunt faces and ragged clothes made discerning their exact ages difficult. The girl's hand clamped over the younger boy's mouth, her eyes wide and knuckles white. He struggled against her, his eyes blinking rapidly and fixed on Samantha like he was set to bolt and run away. Tears cut cracks through the dirt on their cheeks.

Samantha motioned a finger to her lips and stood up again. She glanced over her shoulder. Biggs was looking straight at her.

"Find something, Henderson?" he asked, his voice straining through his clenched teeth.

"No, Sir." She looked him straight in the eye and squared her shoulders, then shifted her weapon back under her arm.

"I don't believe you." He walked briskly to her position, his mouth twisted into a scowl.

"It's just animals, Biggs. Groundhogs. Get hold of yourself."

"Shut the fuck up, Henderson. We all know you're a traitor." He pushed her aside and stooped down. "You got me some little ones. I fucking hate the kids, but I like it when they scream."

As he began to draw his weapon, Samantha spun around and pointed her gun at him. "You're not killing them, Biggs. They're innocent children. Look at them. It's clear to anyone with a brain that they're not infected." The words seemed to stumble out of her mouth, but the resolve inside her was very real. A fire burned inside her chest—a flame she'd only experienced in the trance of painting.

"Traitor!" He lunged at her, bellowing his rage as he brought his own weapon the bear.

Without thinking, she pointed her gun at his head and fired. "Run, now!" she screamed into the bush as Biggs' head exploded, showering her in his inhuman blood and brains and shards of shattered bone. The taste of copper assaulted her as a chunk of gore splattered against her mouth.

The children sprinted out of the bushes and into the corn, just as Biggs' headless body collapsed in a heap at her feet. Her chest heaved as she drew in breath after breath, and she dropped her gun on the ground and clenched her shaking hands together. The metallic taste of blood spread through her mouth and filled her senses, then she took a few steps before her legs collapsed beneath her. Her stomach turned, ejecting her breakfast of oatmeal over Biggs' corpse.

The thud of boots barely registered as the men surrounded her, or the grip of the hands that restrained her. She grinned up at the sunless sky, past their angry faces.

She knew she'd done the right thing.

Chapter 15

The leather full-body restraints bit into Samantha's skin as she awoke, and her head hurt. She blinked against the harsh lights of the medical bay and her nostrils were filled with the stench of hyper-sterility. As her vision cleared and the tranquilizer-induced haze left her, she lifted her head with some difficulty and looked into the frowning face of her commander. Against the clean white background, she could have almost mistaken him for an angel in some televised rendition of heaven, if she believed in such things.

"You killed him, Sammy." Remus McIntyre spoke, his frown deep enough to crease his brow and forehead.

"I did it for those innocent kids, Captain." The old conviction had come back, although her voice betrayed her. Her mouth tasted of old blood and metal.

"We found no sign of any children, Sammy. Just you and Biggs."

"He was going to kill them, I told them to run. What he was doing was wrong, Captain. There are survivors." A tear leaked down her face. She wished she could have brought the two orphans to the base, fed them back to health and taken care of them.

The captain only nodded, his eyes held downcast.

"The little girl put her hand over the boy's mouth to keep him from screaming. Zombies don't do that. They wouldn't be hiding in bushes and starving to death while we steal their food!" Samantha screamed.

"I believe you, Sammy."

"Then what do we do?" she asked, choking back a sob.

"I don't know, Sammy. Do I risk everyone here for a few strays? Do I let my people kill innocents?" He picked up a tissue and dabbed her eyes with it.

"We have to do something, Sir." More tears rolled down her face, and she struggled against the restraints.

"I know." His voice had become barely a whisper. "But you killed a man, a comrade, Sammy. I can't ignore that, either. We'll talk again, after I've sorted this out," He said, his voice returning to its usual volume.

"I understand, Sir."

The captain took a few steps back, and spoke to his aide. Then a pair of orderlies rolled her back to the adjoining cell block.

They unhooked the restraints, pushed her into the cell, and immediately lowered the transparent metal barrier. An orange uniform lay on the steel bench, the only thing with color in the small drab cell. Samantha snatched it up and pitched it against the wall. "Damnit!" she yelled.

Taking a deep breath, she got down on the floor. The captain would be back for her—she needed to keep herself in top shape until he did.

She began doing pushups.

One, two, three, four...

Low Orbit

(Low Orbit was published in the February 2012 edition of Sirens Call Magazine as part of Women in Horror Month. The story idea itself arose when someone asked if The ABACUS Protocol had zombies in it. Zombies, on a space station? Challenge accepted.)

Captain Tony Connor floated in the middle of the room, his eyes fixed on the view screens that offered him an unparalleled view of the Earth. His space station was small, only a simple cylinder divided into three rooms—a test design for a new, larger research station. The once-polished metal walls were smeared with handprints, and a few of the lights lining the ceiling had flickered out, causing the handrails mounted onto the walls for easy zero-g navigation to cast shadows at eerie angles. Tony had trained his entire post-adolescent life for an opportunity of this magnitude, but the experience was nothing like he'd hoped it would be. Since the *incident*, he'd spent the past forty days alone, a sentinel watching over a world that no longer spoke to him. The last time he'd been in contact with mission control, he'd heard only screams, followed by the silent embrace of the dead vacuum of space. The Internet that connected his new prototype space station with the world had been severed soon after. He left the communication lines open, and he'd taken to talking to himself, often and at length. This semblance of normalcy was all that came between him and the disconcerting conclusion that he was alone. The void of space didn't care what happened to him, but maybe someone out there did. He'd even come to long for the jeers of the night controller, Sylvain, who always asked him if he was ready to be the last human left alive. Tony had made a mental note to punch that jackass as soon as he got home.

It seemed that bad joke had come true, but Tony still wanted to punch the guy right in his fat face.

Earth was his only friend now, and she had changed dramatically. During every night orbit, the bright cities, monuments to humanity's greatness and tenacity, grew dimmer. Eventually, the brightest lights winked out, leaving the smaller cities and towns defiant against the engulfing darkness. In the past week, the final sets of lights in Australia had winked out one by one. When his orbit swung to the dark side of the earth, not even the faint lights of the most distant stars could quell the rumbling of his gut.

Now, the Earth had left him too. Her night-side was as barren and bereft of light as the blackest pit. Tony swallowed, hard, as his desperate eyes sought out any remaining point—any bastion of residual hope. He held a trembling finger to his mouth, and began to gnaw on his index finger. All his fingers were marked with scabs and scars—as his food supplies waned, he'd embraced any distraction to the hunger that waged war in his belly. The patchiness of hair on his scalp evidenced the terrible necessity that his slow starvation demanded—anything to fill the growling void inside.

Blood danced across his tongue, the coppery taste shooting him back to reality. His weak legs propelled him off the wall, towards the colorful computer terminal—his peripheral vision had noted a quick blip tracking across the screen. A desperate need drove him to check the radio and internet connections, even if the signals and shipments were only figments of his imagination. A sense of futility had him plucking a hair from his scalp and feeding it to his eager mouth. His water supply had grown stagnant, and the air scrubbers were almost a month overdue for changing. The food supplies hadn't fared much better, though it was easier to ration food than air or water. With every motion, his body odor wafted into his nostrils. Scrunching up his face against the smell, he plucked another hair, noting with some satisfaction that it was one of the grey ones that had been plaguing him for his entire adult life, and popped it into his mouth.

Swirling the coarse hair around his tongue, Tony brought up the familiar controls. He clamped his eyes shut and counted to ten. The hair cut into the soft flesh of his tongue, but he didn't care.

The station lurched for an instant, and Tony's eyes blinked open. It hadn't been a hallucination. Something had docked. Saliva rushed to his mouth at the thought of more ration packs. Clean water. A fresh uniform. He swallowed the hair and propelled himself towards the claustrophobic space that served as a docking bay. Its contents and stores were long depleted, leaving empty metal boxes strapped to the wall. The too-bright lights glared off of every metal surface. He laughed and spun through the air as he approached the door, for once oblivious to the room's emptiness. The sounds caught in his throat, until a good clearing loosened them.

"You had me worried, there!" he said, relief washing over him. "I thought you'd forgotten about me. Man, I hope you guys get the lights turned on back home, it's damn depressing to look at from up here." He moved forwards, swinging and propelling himself from beam to beam to reach the airlock. The door remained shut; its passenger or cargo unable to enter the proper codes.

"Codes were a stupid idea," he said as he pressed the opening sequence into the keypad. "As if I'm going to blow my stupid ass into space." His shaking hands keyed in the wrong code, again. After a deep sigh, he held his breath, and focused on the buttons, imagining food, proper hygiene and clean water. Those simple necessities could inspire anyone.

The door rolled open and a new stench assailed his nostrils. The pungent smell of decay caused his throat to constrict and his eyes to bulge. It should be impossible, but a *person* was hunched over inside the pod.

"Sylvain?" The word barely escaped his lips before his corpulent supervisor turned to face him. His cheap polyester suit was in tatters and stiff with dried blood. He'd put on even more weight since Tony had last seen him. But, the man's face told a different story. It wasn't Sylvain—not anymore. The man's lips had curled back in a savage grimace. His face and lips were smeared with gore. His eyes stared out, but there was no recognition in them.

The thing that Sylvain had become floated in mid-air, then its arm reached to grasp at him. Tony flew back against the bulkhead, recoiling from the man's ruined fingers. The left middle finger was torn away at the second knuckle; the other fingernails were peeled back from the flesh, bent at painful and unnatural angles.

Tony froze while he stared at what remained of his boss. The creature moved with little concern for its own injuries, Sylvain had been trained in space movement, but this thing was unable to comprehend the logistics of moving in zero gravity.

Tony knew he could jettison the pod and have it tumble back to Earth. His eyes flickered across the boxes of supplies that were stacked inside. He imagined them packed full of food, clean water, maybe even a letter from his family.

A rattling snarl snapped him back into reality. A spray of weightless spittle sent him recoiling into the main room. His eyes, now wide with desperation, searched the walls and his living quarters for something—anything— that could be used as a weapon. His breathing clattered in his ears, and the musky air was made richer by Sylvain's stench. Tony blinked away the tears that blurred his vision, then his eyes focused on the single loose handrail. He pushed himself towards it with all his remaining strength, and his trembling hands closed around it. Sylvain had never sent him the glue or brackets needed to have it fixed, claiming that it was too dangerous for Tony to attempt the repair on his own.

Tony slid his hand down the familiar metal. He'd wedged an empty plastic food pack into the gap in the place of glue, to keep the bar in place when he needed to use it. A string of blood-thirsty howls drifted in from the storage area. As he shuddered in response, his fingers slipped off the plastic wedge before they could get a solid grip. He glanced to the adjoining room just as the thing drifted head over heels once again. There was still time. What if Sylvain figured out how to move in zero gravity?

Tony dried his damp fingers on his pants leg, and tried again. His broken fingernails burned against the pressure, but at last the plastic snapped free and he was able to slide the bar out of place. It was hollow lightweight aluminum, and only about a meter long. But in the absence of anything better, it would have to do.

He clenched the weapon in his trembling hand, and then he swung himself across the lab, back into the storage area. His breath came in ragged pants and his heart pounded so hard he thought it might explode. Fear wouldn't save him, so he swallowed- it back, hard, and went in to do whatever was necessary. He wasn't going to let Sylvain hold him hostage until his hunger claimed him.

Sylvain hung in the air, almost where Tony had left him. Droplets of spit hovered everywhere, and Tony shuddered. Saliva had always caused disgust to sour his stomach, and now was no exception. He forced himself to focus on Sylvain's bloated face and mangled mouth. With a cry, he propelled himself towards the man.

His approach seemed to take an eternity. He watched as the thing's arms snatched wildly at the air in front of him, and bile rose in his throat as he saw more fluid gush from hideous mouth. Sylvain took a swing with the metal bar—but the creature managed to grab it in one hand and pull Tony towards him.

In a panic, Tony snatched a nearby handlebar with his other hand, pulling back with what was left of his waning strength. Lights flashed before his eyes as a hard tug from the other end threatened to dislocate his shoulder.

Every action has an equal and opposite reaction.

Newton's third law passed through his mind, and his eyes widened in understanding.

An object in motion stays in motion, unless acted on by an outside force.

His face contorted into an unfamiliar grin.

Pulling back as hard as he could, he rooted his feet to the closest support—a cargo container. Another agonizing jolt ripped through his torso.

With a scream, he pushed back towards the far wall. Sylvain came with him, hissing and flailing. Letting the pole drop, Tony grabbed the next handle and pressed himself tight against the wall. Sylvain flew past, his bawling and struggling rendering him impotent. He hadn't let go of the pipe.

Sylvain collided with the wall, and crumpled against it. Rancid air gushed from the thing's lungs, and his head now hung at a sickening angle. Tony assessed the situation: his only route of escape was blocked, and now the creature had Tony's only weapon.

As Tony's mind scrambled for a plan, Sylvain managed to turn to face him, his vacant dead eyes locking onto Tony's.

Sylvain then pushed off the wall.

Tony screamed with the realization of what this meant. His heart seemed to pause for an instant before he threw himself at the supply pod's open door. If that thing had learned how to move on zero gravity, there was no hope for him.

His quivering hands jammed against the door code. Twice wrong. Sylvain was getting close—Tony could almost feel his fetid, burning breath fouling his skin, the little droplets of moisture coating him with whatever it was that turned him.

Eyes wide, he tried the code again.

The doors slammed shut, then the dull sound of the docking clamps releasing signaled that the pod had detached.

"Good luck with being the last man alive," he whispered.

Then he gazed at the crates of supplies.

If he didn't survive re-entry, at least he wasn't going to die hungry. It was time to feast.

Radio Silence

(Radio Silence was published in August 2014 as part of the Fading Hope anthology by Autumnal Press. This anthology's purpose was to write the bleakest fiction imaginable. This was originally a story idea for the main Zombie Bedtime Stories storyline. I cut it because it didn't do anything further the plot.)

Michael pulled the clock key from around his neck, its tarnished brass a dull green in the candle's flickering light. The thin leather cord that tied it around his neck dangled limply from the keyhole, its frayed edges caressing the metal. Smoke from the old wood stove tickled his nose, and he sucked in a deep breath and held it as he let the stillness of the world settle into him. For six months, he'd maintained the ritual of keeping time. Years before, he'd wound his uncle's clock out of duty and obligation. Now, it was different obligation that spurred him forwards. A need for order.

He exhaled as his thick, veiny fingers slid the key into the hole on the front of the antique clock, an heirloom inherited from his long-dead uncle. Rich varnish meshed with the cast iron moldings, peaking in knotted wood carving forgotten by modern designers. By some miracle, he'd been able to turn off the chime without damaging the myriad of spinning gears and levers inside. He couldn't let them hear.

Sucking in another breath, he turned the key clockwise, listening intently to the sounds outside the room as he twisted. Everyone upstairs was still asleep—the next watch wouldn't start for another hour.

He twisted the key again and again, until at last the clock was wound. "That's another month we've got," Michael muttered under his breath. The rest remained unsaid: If we're not dead first.

He replaced the key around his neck, tucking it beneath the lapels of his plaid flannel shirt. Michael then turned to face the room, his ritual completed. His small cottage—his sanctuary-turned-prison had seen better days. Dated wood paneling covered the walls, floors, and ceilings. The windows were blocked by an assortment of bedding, burlap sacks, and even cobbled together plastic shopping bags. A tear came to his eye when his gaze came to the solid wooden bookshelves—his vaunted collection of literature. The shelves were now packed with whatever food they could find. The books were nothing more than a memory of warmth on a cold winter's morning. Michael longed to curl up in his bed and let a classic take him to another time, or escape with something modern. But now, all he had to read were food tins and radio manuals.

Michael shook his head, and the memories of happier days and good books dissipated. He walked over to the sink, and smiled as water once again greeted him. Gratified that his years of resisting upgrading the cottage's well had turned out for the best, he filled a pot of water and set it on the wood stove. Jacob wasn't any good to anyone before he'd had his morning coffee. Of course, coffee was just a memory now, unless they had a lucky scavenging run. But, it seemed that dried chicory root or tea would do in a pinch.

Michael's neck turned at the sound of gentle footfalls coming from above. He stretched and rolled his shoulders, pushing his hands into the aura of warmth surrounding the wood stove.

"Hey, old man," said a deep voice held just above a whisper. "Where's my damn coffee?"

Michael turned and nodded at the young man, just shy of twenty five. His dark eyes latched onto Michael's, and flashed him a predatory grin, teeth white against the beginnings of a patchy beard. Jacob was among the youngest of their band of survivors, but Michael knew him to be as calm and controlled as any elder. "Coming right up," he replied in a hushed voice.

Jacob crossed from the stairs to the kitchen and took down his favorite mug—an old souvenir from Alcatraz. Michael had visited over a decade ago, and brought the mug back to the cabin as a souvenir. Now, Jacob refused to use any other cup. He then glided over to the empty bookshelf and retrieved a yellow tin.

Jacob turned and examined the just-steaming pot of water. He pursed his lips as he spooned a crumbly brown substance into the cup. "Looks like Priss and I need to go do some shopping," he said.

Michael rubbed his forehead with the back of his hand, and shivered. "It's not too soon?" he asked, leaving out the end of the question: After we lost Suzanne. That had been a productive raid, but where three had left, only two returned.

Jacob chortled and hefted the pot off the stove just as the bubbles began to break the surface. "Doesn't matter if it's too soon or not, old man," he said as he swirled the murky contents of the cup. "Grass grows, birds shit, and I need a decent fucking cup of coffee." He sniffed the contents of the cup and scrunched up his face.

Michael shook his head and sighed.

Jacob took a swig of the homebrew and grimaced. "Yup. That settles it. We're totally going to visit Wayne Jones' farmhouse. If I have to drink this shit, I'm going to eat good meat."

"You don't mean the pig farmer's, do you?" Michael asked. He'd talked to Wayne over the CB radio, until the power went out and the generator's ensuing power surge had fried the unit. Jacob and Priss had visited his farm soon after, but without the proper supplies and technical know-how, the radio would never work again.

"Yeah, why not? Bonus if the old fart's still alive, but..." Jacob paused to take another gulp of his drink, "But, ya' know, free pork either way, right?"

Michael nodded. Their last visit to Wayne's had resulted in some fifty pounds of salted and desiccated meat, just after the radio had failed. The thought of a good slab of meat made him salivate. "You can't be taking him for granted, Jacob," he said, before shaking his head, "but, I won't say no to free meat."

"I knew you'd come around," Jacob said. He chugged the rest of his drink in one fluid motion, and wiped his mouth with the back of his hand. "So, I'm thinking that me and Priss will set out at dawn, tomorrow. We gotta get our things together. It's about a three hour walk out to Wayne's digs, and four back if he sends us loaded up."

"You're not taking the main roads, are you?" Michael asked. That was how they'd lost Suzanne, and the others.

"Not this time," Jacob said, setting his cup down on the wooden kitchen table. "I think we've learned better than to take the easy way. Buggers don't like to be alone in the woods."

"Okay, fine. I'll make sure you've got provisions for the day during my watch." Michael rubbed his eyes, trying to massage away the dull ache building in his sinuses. Getting old sucked. Getting old in a dusty cabin with no good food sucked even more.

"Sounds good to me. Thanks, old man." Jacob mock-saluted and then dropped down into the kitchen chair, swinging his feet up onto the table. "Now, get your ass to bed before it gets cold."

Michael touched two fingers to his brow and moved towards the worn wooden steps. His hand seized the banister and he hauled himself upwards, one step at a time. The air cooled with every step away from the wood stove. He opened the first door on the right and tip-toed over the sleeping forms huddled on the floor, until he reached the bed. Dropping into the still-warm embrace of the blankets, he closed his eyes and allowed sleep to wash over him.

There was blood everywhere. Limbs spurting gouts of blood. Blood become raindrops and pattering on the ground. It was on Michael's hands, working itself into the aged grooves of his skin. His nails were black and clotted with it. The smell of copper stung his nose and worked its way into his mouth. Saliva and bile gushed forwards, but not before the screams started.

Michael sat bolt upright in his tiny cot, his skin beading with cold sweat. The dreams of before the cataclysm that had torn the world into little pieces always ended with the screams. At first, they were his friend's screams, as distinct and unique as each of them had been. But, as time marched on, their voices had melted into a singular dread chorus. He checked his hands, quickly, just to be sure. They were clean of blood. But, the memory of his labors over their lifeless forms persisted. A tourniquet sealing the raw meat of a severed limb. Pressure on a seeping bite wound. One by one, they'd dropped into a deep sleep… followed by the nothingness of a temporary death.

Michael shut his eyes, and sucked in a deep breath. He forced the air from his lungs, before dragging in another deep inhalation. He clenched his teeth. *No, I will not remember this,* he thought. But, their pale forms still swung listlessly in the eternal focus of his mind's eye.

He swung one leg over the side of the bed, then another. His back and his hips expressed their typical geriatric neediness. He dismissed them, with more success than he'd had vanquishing the ghosts of his fallen comrades.

He might not be able to help them, not after all this time. His friends were likely still out there in the woods, lost and alone. Lost and screaming. But, he knew he could get Wayne's radio working again.

Wayne's voice wouldn't be warped into screams. Not like them.

Not like them, memory whispered in agreement.

Michael pulled himself to the small chest of drawers his father had made as a youth. His shaking hands reached towards the unfinished, wooden drawers, quiet and determined. Silence was a skill to be embraced. It let the sleepers continue with their rest, and it kept the others from finding them during the long nights. Michael never thought he'd be nostalgic for the pervasive light pollution that had plagued this portion of the continent. At least you could see. The stars were cold comfort when they shrouded fiends.

He drew out some clothes—a faded plaid jacket and a ragged pair of jeans. Michael turned them over as he changed so he wouldn't see the stain that still graced the backside of the pants. That was all he had left of Sharon.

Or, was it his precious Jillian? That fateful evening was still a blur, further obscured by the fog of time. His trembling hands withdrew a faded army green knapsack, its narrow armbands frayed and coated in the grime of his juvenile handprints. He discarded his worn clothes in a heap at the foot of the bed. Someone on cleaning duty would tend to them later.

Michael straightened, rolling his shoulder back until a pop could be heard. The relief was short lived, however. He looked back for a moment before making his way down the old staircase.

Sunlight crept through the cracks in the blinds, fingers of light caressing furniture and illuminating the particles of dust that floated through the air. A deep inhale unsettled the dust, sending it swirling through the room. The kitchen was devoid of life—Jacob had likely started his morning squirrel hunt and the early risers were usually in the garden.

Michael moved to the desk in the corner, and sat down in front of his faithful radio. Its once bright polish was now tarnished, and long hours had worn finger imprints into the controls. He settled the familiar headphones over his ears and flicked it on, the hum reassuring him that his last connection to the outside world still operated. His fingers danced over dials as he went through the motions of scanning through the frequencies, searching for word on other survivors. At last, he tuned in to Wayne's preferred frequency, and waited.

Leaving the headphones on, he opened a drawer. Often on his long nights alone, he thought of every possible malfunction that could knock out a radio. Michael didn't have a spare antenna, but he was sure that he had spares of just about every other part. He'd made sure to visit electronics stores during the first few raids they'd made on the city, before the Army had begun exterminating civilians and looting the stores themselves. Now, it was too risky to leave the country retreat and they'd been forced to improvise. Michael had listened to the carnage as an invisible spectator—bearing witness to the end of freedom, decency, and human life. Even Jacob understood that the city was off-limits until the marauders moved on.

Michael's hands moved from part to part. He checked the connections to be sure they were free of corrosion and packed them into a small plastic tackle box he's repurposed for storing electronics. The red box had a handle, but was small enough to easily fit into his knapsack. Perspiration stuck to his brow and moistened the limp remains of his once proud head of hair. He sniffed and pursed his lips as he finished packing the colorful little parts and wires into their container. Then, he rummaged around the bottom of the drawer until he withdrew a soldering iron, some solder, and one of his precious remaining packs of batteries. His fingers hesitated for a moment before dropping the latter into the bag. Then, he tucked the tackle box in on top of it and stood up. For an instant, his fingers curled around the key dangling from his neck. The leather dug into the skin of his neck and the metal was warm against the palm of his hand. For a moment, he wondered what his uncle would have done. But, he shook his head and dismissed the thought. His uncle would have kept the clock running, not go off on a crazy mission to fix a radio.

Michael sighed. He slung the backpack over his shoulder and turned towards the front porch. He could at least enjoy the afternoon sunlight while he waited for Jacob to get back. His bones creaked their agreement and he plodded towards the door.

***

Michael took a deep breath, his nostrils flaring against the morning air. Still laden with dew, it carried to him smells of rotting leaves and fresh pine. He squinted at the distance, forcing the trail into focus. Dampness clung to him like a second skin, but he didn't complain. At least he had been allowed to come along—to be useful.

They had been walking in silence for what seemed like hours. His leg creaked as he stepped over yet another fallen tree. Mud clung to his worn boots. He raised a hand to swat a mosquito when something caught his eye in the distance. Something grey—about the size of a man, but wasted and lean.

His feet stuck to the ground, as though his muscles couldn't decide if they wanted to freeze him into a statue or send him flying into the woods like a doe. It rustled in the trees behind him. He spun in a fluid motion that belied his age to face it. His eyes widened as memory flooded his reality with images of Jillian, her leg ripped from the cradle of its socket, crawling towards him. Her large blue eyes pleaded for him to make her whole again. Thick brown hair tattered and out of place. Calling his name—calling for the father who couldn't save her.

A hand clapped against his back, and he jumped. Heart racing and blood pounding through his ears, he turned. Jacob squinted at him, before shaking his head. Priss—a young woman with stringy hair and a tattered nostril which had once held a nose ring rolled her eyes and turned away. A scowl had been etched on her face for as long as he'd known her, drawing harsh lines on her supple skin. Something about Priss made his skin crawl.

"Shit, old timer," Jacob said in a low voice, shaking his head. "At least we know your hearing is still good!"

"Shh!" Priss growled, her eyes narrowing into slits.

"Whatever, Priss. It's a fucking squirrel." Jacob took Michael by the crook of the elbow and led him further down the path before continuing. "I don't know why I put up with that woman. Freaks out over squirrels and fucking gets me into all kinds of trouble. You know what I mean, Mikey?"

Michael only shook his head. He looked back to where he'd seen the figure, but the trees had moved. He raised a trembling hand to point to where it used to be. He drew in breath after rattling breath, but only the sound of the desperate rushing of his own blood reached his ears.

Jacob peered back in the direction of Michael's outstretched finger. His head cocked and his eyes narrowed. "Priss!" he hissed in little more than a whisper as he hefted the solid stick he carried into both hands.

Priss glared at him, the grimace turning her features to stone.

A screeching howl cut through the air. Michael's heart skipped a beat, and renewed memories of blood and gore played through his mind. It was one of them! A fiend—one of the formerly human inhabitants of this valley—had found their safe trail!

"Run!" Jacob shoved Michael down the trail with a force that threatened to bring the old man to his knees.

Michael recovered, and sprinted down the trail. His knapsack bounced as he ran, the heavy tackle box smacking into his aching lower back. He shot past trees and over mud puddles in his mad dash away from it. Another soulless scream shattered the tranquility of the forest path.

Footsteps sounded behind him. Michael grit his teeth and drove himself further, faster than he'd gone even as a young man playing soccer. He drew in ragged breaths and his legs wobbled, but he maintained the pace.

They turned around a bend in the trail and there it was—Wayne's farmhouse. The gate hung ajar, and the grey wooden fence had collapsed in many places. The grass was overgrown and no smoke curled from the chimney.

Michael found himself slowing, until another scream spurred him forwards again. Jacob said, between pants: "Get inside!"

Pain shot through Michael's feet as he pushed himself through the dilapidated gate. He glanced backwards. An emaciated man—or, what had been a man once—was chasing them. His grey skin was stretched over his bones, and most of his hair had fallen out. A gash in his scalp displayed an arch of sun bleached bone. Michael screamed, his breath hot and metallic, and put on one final burst of speed.

The door fell off the hinges as he barreled through it, so he took shelter in the next room. Jacob stopped and readied the heavy stick. Priss had drawn a rusty old machete from her pack. Jacob took a step forward, bellowing as his staff connected with the thing's head. Paper-thin skin split open, and its face sloughed down over its chest as the living corpse tumbled to the ground. Priss stepped forward with the nimbleness of a dancer, bringing the heavy blade over the thing's neck in one fell swoop.

It was over. Michael took a deep, shaking breath. His whole body shook. He took an uneven step towards the front door when his left foot hit something and sent it clattering across the wooden floor. His eyes traced its motion. It was off-white with defined hard edges. A glance around the room showed that something had happened here. The furniture was not as he remembered it. It was stained with water, or perhaps something else? Isolation could do funny things to people. He walked after the spinning object, and gasped.

It was a chunk of bone. But why was there bone in the house? Wayne wasn't the type to bring his work home with him. Squatting, he picked it up. He spun it through his shaking fingers, peering at the smoothness of the break. The roughness of its core scraped against his weathered skin. He let it fall to the floor.

"You home, Wayne?" he called out. His voice wheezed.

After waiting a few moments for a reply, he glanced back at the door. He then drew off his backpack, and fumbled with the handle of his tackle box before pulling it free. If memory served, the radio was in the kitchen. He picked his way past a shattered coffee table. His eyes scanned the walls and windows. The wallpaper was faded, its vertical stripes marred by cracks and scuffs. He paused mid-step, and listened. Jacob was cursing somewhere in the distance. There were no other sounds other than the rustle of leaves and Michael's heaving breaths. He shrugged. Perhaps Wayne was in the barn, tending to his small army of hogs.

He crossed the threshold into the kitchen, and he let his eyes scan the room as he bent over, hands on his aching knees. A dank musk assailed his nostrils. Sweat clung to his eyelids. Michael tried to rub the moisture from his brow with the back of his hand, but he only succeeded in getting the salty liquid into his eyes.

Blinking, he focused on a wooden school desk in the corner, next to the counter. The counter was covered in plastic bins, each heaped high with salt. His stomach grumbled at the suggestion of food, but he ignored it—there was time for a snack later. He pulled the worn office chair back from the desk, his fingers melding into the exposed yellow padding. He placed the tackle box on the chair's cracked fabric seat before examining the radio.

When he flipped the power switch, the lights winked to life.

He pursed his lips, and began turning the dials. All seemed to be in order. He shook his head, and he stretched over the radio, peering behind it. His shaking fingers traced each wire to its proper connection. Michael's grasping reached the sharp cut of metal. He gasped and pulled his hand back, staring at the droplet of blood that had welled up on his right index finger.

The injured finger went into his mouth. He grimaced at the coppery taste as he sucked. Why would the wire be cut? He squatted down, and squinted under the desk. Underneath, two wires lay on the floor. Their twisted copper innards were cut, creating a nest of metal.

Michael tried to stand. He gulped down air, the contents of his stomach churning against gravity. His eyes caught another glint of white, and he cried out. A pair of human skulls, broken and missing the jaws, sat under the kitchen table. Michael's legs collapsed out from under him, and he landed on his tailbone, hard. One of the skulls was completely cleaned of flesh, while the other had some tendrils of gore still clinging to it. His eyes widened.

Footsteps echoed behind him. "I was hoping you wouldn't see this, old man," Jacob said.

Michael's mouth was too tired to articulate more than one word. "Why?"

"Well, y'see, humans are edible too. That fucker wouldn't give us meat, so we put in a change of ownership."

Bile rose to Michael's mouth. His eyes spun around, and rested on the pristine radio sitting in the corner of the room.

A sharp pain connected with the back of Michael's head. Blackness followed. The last thing he heard was Jillian's voice. *Daddy?*

The Zombie's Bride

(I wrote this for fun soon after finishing Locked In. It received mixed reviews—people who like gory zombie stories loved it, people looking for zombie-themed erotica hated it. Can't please everyone.)

Julia pursed her lips as she stared into the mirror. She couldn't get her earrings to hang right. She couldn't believe after how much she'd spent on them that they couldn't even point down properly. She pouted and turned to her maid of honor, Sarah "Oh my God these earrings are going to ruin my whole wedding!" she said. Julia had spent weeks and more money than her credit cards would allow on this, and it had to be perfect! She had even joined a gym and worked hard so she could squeeze into the largest size her dream wedding gown would come in.

Sarah rolled her eyes. "Everything is going to ruin your wedding. First the cake, then you needed to lose fifty pounds, then the bridesmaids not wanting to wear those hideous dresses that were not only blue and turquoise but also had horizontal stripes. Get over it already! Ugh." Sarah's voice cracked. Sarah was awkward—tall and skinny.

"I want to be the most beautiful girl at my own wedding; is that so much to fucking ask?" Julia said as she snorted, flaring her wide, flat nose.

"I want to be able to show people those pictures, not hide them in my closet!" Sarah said.

"Then find a man who will spend more than one night with you and get married you dumb slut."

Julia looked forward to not having to spend as much time with Sarah. She only put up with Sarah because she made her look graceful, and because her first choice had vanished from the face of the Earth.

"You are such a fat cow. I bet he cheats on you within a year." Sarah stuck out her tongue.

Julia lamented having to replace Haley as her maid of honor, but she stopped answering her phone at the last minute. At least her dress fit Sarah. While she hated Haley for being a too-good perfect girl who also had the audacity to be good looking and have a handsome boyfriend, at least Haley never called her fat.

"God you are such a bitch, I think you just—" she began, cut off by her ringing phone. She answered it while Sarah rolled her eyes like a petulant child. "What?" It was her fiancé. He told her there had been a fight at his bachelor party, and he and his friends had been attacked by a crazed person on the street.

"What the fuck is wrong with you! You know it's bad luck for us to be together or even talk before the wedding! You're ruining this for me! You're ruining our marriage and our relationship and how could you be so fucking stupid?" Julia screamed into the phone. She watched as Sarah giggled. Of course that skinny cow wouldn't understand real love.

"Well, I thought you might want to know. We need to go to the hospital and—,"he stammered into the phone.

"You are not postponing our wedding after I have worked this hard! You're not going to ruin this again, I don't care, you will be there or I will never forgive you!" Julia finished before slamming down the receiver.

"Can you believe that dick? He wanted to postpone

the ceremony because his friend got bitten by a crazy woman."

Sarah only laughed.

***

The next morning she woke up bloated from all the chocolate she'd eaten to comfort herself. Wedging herself into her dress was an almost insurmountable challenge, but eventually, she crammed herself into the tight gown and waited while her hair, makeup and other grooming was done to perfection. Even her earrings hung right. She waited for her father to arrive with his Cadillac to take them to the scenic lake they'd reserved for the ceremony. She waited. He arrived on time.

"How could you not be early, Dad? You're going to ruin it all!" she said, annoyed at his lack of consideration.

"Sorry, darling. I know it's your special day," he said, his voice quiet and thoughtful. When he glanced at his watch to check the time, she realized his timing had been perfect.

"Oh I'm sorry, Daddy. You know how much I love you, right?"

"Of course I do, sweetie." He returned to driving, and watched the road in silence.

They came up to the lakeside resort. Tethered balloons floated from the fence posts along the way. Julia wasn't impressed. She remembered asking for foil balloons, not little kid birthday balloons! They turned the corner, and she screamed. "This place is a mess! It's all ruined!" The decorations had been ripped down, picnic tables and chairs were overturned and the windows of the lodge were broken. "Oh my God! Daddy, what happened?"

"I don't know sweetie. Stay in the car; I'm going to make some calls." He brought the car to idle by the road and took out his phone. Julia sat and stared out the window. A figure moved, and caught her eye. It was John, her fiancé. He was wearing a white tuxedo and stood facing the water. Enraged, she unlocked the door and stepped outside.

"Darling, no!" her father said, his eyes going wide.

"It's okay Daddy. I see John and I am going to get an explanation for this right now!" She hurried out the door and slammed it shut, jamming her long white dress in the door. "Oh fuck, not my dress!" Tears came to her eyes as she opened the door and pulled the dress out. A long crease marred the dress' white silk, and mascara melted across the back of her hand when she wiped away her tears. She marched towards the lake. Rage emanated from her pores along. This was all John's fault!

"John, you dumb fucker! You've ruined my special day! How could you let it get like this!"

John turned to face her. He was pale, and blood was smeared all over his face. His handsome white tuxedo was coated in drying blood, already turning brown. "Oh my God, I told you we are *not* having a stupid theme wedding. And we have to return that tux! What were you thinking?"

There was no reply, only a loud, inhuman roar. He ran towards her, mouth agape. She took a step back, and tripped over her dress. Julia fell onto her back. She rolled from side to side, trying to gain some purchase to right herself. The, she heard the unmistakable sound of ripping fabric.

"You bastard, you made me ruin my dress!" Julia screamed as she threw her hands in front of her face.

He crashed into her, mouth wide and teeth bared. He smelled of blood. Dark chunks of something were stuck between his teeth.

"Daddy help me!" she yelled. Pain overwhelmed

her as John sank his filthy teeth into her chest just below her collarbone. She tried to push his head away, but the struggle was futile. He was too strong. She could see the best man running towards them along the beach, like a knight ready to save her.

"Help me Carl!"

Carl looked at her and shrieked as John ripped another mouthful of flesh from her chest. But Carl didn't stop; he pounced on her like an animal.

"No! Stop!" She wheezed out another breath. The corset wasn't letting her breathe! She could hear her father's voice calling to her from somewhere in the distance.

Carl tore a chunk of flesh from her throat. A spray of blood splattered against the sand and her beautiful organza dress. Her arms went weak as John leaned in and tore the flesh from her round cheeks. Tears streamed down her face and mixed with the rivulets of blood that were now flowing from her wounds. She was so dizzy and tired. The mouthfuls of flesh they hewed from her didn't hurt anymore, but the betrayal did.

Before everything went black, her last thoughts were about how John had ruined her special day.

Zombie Pride

(I wrote this soon after writing Locked Out. I was going for a theme of awful people receiving poetic justice via zombies.)

The steering wheel was slick with Rex Parson's sweat. He was a stout, rotund little man. He wore oversized sunglasses that dominated the upper-half of his face. The hot sun bore into him, but he was excited to do God's work. He was a preacher in a small town church, and he was known for his strength of faith and conviction that homosexuality could be cured through prayer. As he drove to the city's first annual Gay Pride parade, he a quiver of trepidation ran through his gut. The blatant immorality had to be stopped, and he was the one who was going to show those vile homosexuals that God was to be feared!

He reflected on the hours he'd spent alone at his computer, researching the complete moral degradation that was present at any Pride event. The images of the men's perfectly toned, oiled bodies made his heart race, and he'd had trouble looking away from them. He knew the lifestyle was sin, and that it was his place to show the wrongdoers the errors of their ways before they tempted weaker souls. He'd decided to undertake this trip alone. He didn't want to expose his congregation to this blasphemy. This was his trial, his war against the sordid abyss.

Rex expected the worst–a celebration of blatant carnality in defiance of God and all His laws. Rex knew he was the last thing that stood between the average person and acceptance of this abomination. He knew the weak-minded women and children would be easily swayed by the display of rippling, masculine perfection, and they would spread the disease of tolerance and appeasement to the rest of their population. Just as they lead Adam to sin, they would lead society to its secular downfall.

He pulled into an available parking spot about a block from the parade route. He seized his well-worn Bible from the passenger's seat. He would don the armor of God spiritually, but physically, all he had was the Good Book. He would smite any and all who tried to force temptation upon him! He was the last pure soul.

The harsh sun glistened on his balding head. He saw a woman, her exotic costume's wings torn and dragging behind her, running from the parade. She didn't turn to look back. It was a clear sign from God—he was needed here to quell the rampant immortality before more minds fell under the sway of the devil.

He charged to the street corner and looked towards the awesome chaos. Bodies lay trampled in the middle of the streets, and shop windows had been smashed. The bright colors of the parade's decor were strewn across the ground. Rex stepped over a barely-clothed man's battered and bloody body. The man grasped at Rex's leg, but Rex kicked his arm away as he continued towards the epicenter of the strife. He held his Bible tight against his chest, secure in the belief that God would protect him from evil.

A cacophony of terrorized screams echoed around the buildings, the sounds twisting together to become one harmonic, agonized voice. The symphony of horror was punctuated by ghoulish shrieks and howls. A bloody man wearing only black leather chaps leapt from an alleyway and raced towards Rex. "They're coming! Run!" the man cried out breathlessly.

Rex found himself distracted by the man's powerful, intimidating physique before he could bring himself to reply. "God will protect me!" Clearly, this fear and chaos was divine retribution from God. There was no other explanation.

Rex began walking down the alley. There were three figures crouched over a still body. Their backs were turned to him and they moved frantically over the fallen man. He knew this was his time. "Sinners! Repent and open your hearts to our Lord, Jesus Christ!" he shouted, speaking with a familiarity gleaned from performing so many prayer sessions for homosexual deviants. He knew exactly what they needed to hear.

The forms stirred in the distance. They turned to face him. They were all women, hair cropped short and dressed in simple jeans and white t-shirts. Under normal circumstances, Rex would have admonished them for abandoning the femininity that was demanded of them, but not this time. When they stood, they revealed the still-twitching body of a man. Then, they turned their faces, smeared in blood, towards him. They were coated in crimson essence from the neck-down, and it soaked through their t-shirts, which clung to their swaying breasts.

Rex took a step back; his hands trembling as they grasped his heavy Bible. He didn't know what these demon women were, but he knew they weren't of God. "Jesus said: I am the way, the –" Rex began, but he was cut off by their infernal howls. He froze. The sound wasn't natural.

The women ran towards him, leaping over gruesomely disfigured bodies. He raised his Bible; it was the only object he had to defend himself with. One of them pulled ahead of the others. He swung the hefty book, hitting her in the face. She shrieked as she careened into the wall. The others were gaining ground, close behind her. Rex braced himself and readied his Bible for another smite. It had a bloody imprint on it where it hit the first woman's face.

He swung the book with all his strength, grazing a stocky blonde-haired woman. She leapt for him and her weight knocked them both to the ground. Rex's head slam against the pavement, and the impact knocked the wind from his lungs. As he flailed against the formidable strength of his ungodly assailant, his Bible dropped from his left hand. He felt vulnerable and unprotected for the first time in his life.

The second woman, a brunette with large brown eyes dove onto him, immediately sinking her teeth into his exposed throat. Rex tried to scream despite his empty lungs, but he could not. His arms shook, but would not respond to his will. Shivers shot down his spine as the blonde woman shoved her face into his exposed jowls and tore the flesh from his face. He couldn't breathe, and the taste of his own blood crept into his mouth through his ruined face. His world turned red with pain.

Why has God forsaken me?

Thank you for reading!

To keep in touch, please visit my website to sign up for my mailing list, or to join my Patreon for exclusive news and updates on all of my projects.

www.PlanetThea.com

www.PlanetThea.com/newsletter

Twitter: @TheaIsis

Please consider leaving a review for this book. Authors need honest reviews to live.

About the Author:

Thea Gregory is a girl with a physics degree. She loves the dark edges that caress the silver lining of life. Her passions are science fiction, the human condition, and anything that challenges our humanity. Thea loves running, pushups, cooking, and has been known to crochet a thing or two. She has a weakness for gaming and Star Trek. Thea is the author of the Zombie Bedtime Stories, and The ABACUS Protocol. She lives in Montreal with her cat, Bonk.